The Orphic Egg Caper

The Orphic Egg Caper

by

Keith Buckley

¶|
Paragraph Line Books 2020
Oakland, CA

First Printing: 2020
ISBN: 978-1-942086-16-1
PL-128

Paragraph Line Books
Oakland, California

www.paragraphline.com

Cover Art: 21stcenturywombat.com
Back Cover Photograph: Patty Lawson-Buckley

This one's for my chief co-conspirator, Jim Sizemore—
    to crime

Introduction

Let me begin by asserting that I never intended to revisit the Osborne Yesterday files, much less make them available for public consumption. From the moment Osborne proposed hiring me as what he sardonically referred to as "my hagiographer," he provided me with an extensive list of the physical, mental and economic harms he would rain down on myself, my family, my friends, and their family members should a word of his exploits ever appear anywhere in any form. As I already had firsthand knowledge of Yesterday's capacity for abject cruelty and a tendency towards unparalleled violence at the slightest provocation, I gave up any thought of touching these lurid tales once our association came to an end. The graphic threats of mutilation and ruin notwithstanding, I was more than adequately compensated for my ghostwriting as well as my silence. And, as I may later have opportunity to describe, the sometimes fraught partnership with a borderline sociopath unencumbered by traditional notions of morality was not without its benefits.

Suffice to say that I've had no problem remaining taciturn and inscrutable on the subject of Osborne Yesterday for the better part of three decades.

Why then, you might ask yourself, am I reading this dubious and hastily assembled hackery? The quick answer is that I was notified several months ago of Osborne's putative demise. His closest living relative petitioned a court to have Osborne declared dead following his mysterious disappearance in 2014. The relative sent me a copy of the court's order along with a detailed account of this relative's financial straits, which had been compounded by the federal government's flat refusal to pay out on Osborne's pension, his Social Security, or to even acknowledge one Osborne Yesterday had ever existed. The lapse in payments on Osborne's term life policy left the relative all but empty-handed. The only possible remaining asset Osborne could bequeath to his relative was what I had written so many years ago. Osborne had told this relative about our work together but, like all of his other personal belongings, his copy of the files vanished along with his person. After a good deal of tortured correspondence and soul-searching, I agreed to sell a redacted version of one of the first files and give Osborne's unfortunate heir the lion's share of the profits. Thanks to the co-occurrence of my retirement from Indiana University and the outbreak of COVID-19, I had the opportunity to do this one good deed which I imagined, in some small measure, might counterbalance the chaos and destruction Osborne left in his wake.

I will close with the caveat I gave Osborne's relative—and you are probably beginning to suspect why I am being less than transparent about my beneficiary's identity—I make no pretenses about the literary merit or the veracity of what you read on the following pages. My job was primarily that of transcriber, although I was given a narrowly defined license to edit the final product. An overwhelming majority of the text is the verbatim memoir of a notoriously unreliable and often mood-altered narrator. I have changed the names of several persons who expressly wished to remain unidentified, and I have removed or altered the descriptions of any criminal acts for which the statute of limitations has yet to run out. I gave very serious consideration to making more substantial changes because there is a part of me, who is a grandfather, a pacifist, and an unrepentant secular humanist, that questions the entertainment value of such wanton carnage and outright insanity. Then again, perhaps years of dealing with Osborne have also left me a little unencumbered by traditional notions of morality ...

Finally, I would like to ask a favor of you. Not the usual wheedling for positive reviews because, all false modesty aside, I have no illusions on that score. Osborne is far from the only person involved in these chronicles who have journeyed beyond the bardo plane without explanation. If I join the ranks of the disappeared, please join my family in pressuring the federal authorities for a more thorough investigation than Osborne and our other fellows received.

Keith Buckley
Bloomington, Indiana
June-August, 2020

8

Prologue

Let's say you're a biology professor at Indiana University, and you happen to get your jollies doing vivisection on squirrels or jamming electrodes in an owl's brain. Who am I to judge? I've done far worse on Uncle Sam's dime to life forms once capable of ordering a Happy Meal. Anyway, the local chapter of PETA has put out a contract on you, so you've hired a bodyguard. One night, you're leaving Jordan Hall, crossing Third Street on your way to the Atwater Parking Garage. You glance over your shoulder to make sure your guy's got your back. What do you see? A tall, elegant dude wearing a black tux, his perfect teeth gleaming in the sodium vapor streetlights, maybe a ravishing blonde clutching at his arm?

Sorry, pal, but you're hallucinating. Your protection is a short, thin weasel of a man, his bony frame draped in a chutney-stained Penney's trench coat. He's got watery gray eyes, a scar down his left cheek, and a cheap half-chewed cigar hanging out of the corner of his lipless mouth. He's in his late forties, he took a crotch-full of flaming shrapnel during 'Nam, he's worked for several three-letter government agencies, but he never learned how to follow regulations. He knows every low-life dirtbag in Monroe County, including most of the I.U. School of Music faculty, drinks and drugs too much, has the temperament of a schizophrenic rat, and the constancy of a bonobo in heat. If you have a problem that's too hot for the local cops, he's all you've got.

And worse yet, he's me.

My name is Yesterday. Osborne Yesterday. Leastways, that's what my business card says these days and what my birth certificate used to say before it got "lost." The card also says I'm a private investigator. I don't want to waste your time with some intellectual spiel about what I do to turn a buck. My line of work is kind of like proctology—somebody in this town's gotta cut through the crap and get to the bottom of things.

No, it's not a glamorous job, doing background checks on job applications and bogus insurance claims, running skip traces, going undercover at the College Mall to catch a chiseler who's light on her

9

register, tailing some schmuck who's cheating on his wife at the local roacharama, or posing as a topless shoeshine girl at Night Moves Gentlemen's Lounge. And let me tell you, it's hard to keep a smile on your face and warm fuzzies about the human race when you're stopping fists with your front teeth, crowbars with the back of your skull, and steel-plated work boots with the remnants of your testicles. I've eaten and dished out my share of lead, and I'm not afraid to use my trusty Colt 1911 if the situation requires. Especially when the situation involves some goddamn IU coed blasting Paula Abdul out of her Walkman loud enough to hear when I'm driving by.

I've made plenty of enemies in this pus-hole of a burg, and that's why I hired a librarian who moonlights as a wannabe writer to keep track of my casebook. I figure sooner or later one of my long-time adversaries is going to catch up with me. That happens, then Buckley's got the green light to spill all the evidence so I can take the motherfucker down. Even if I'm lying on the roadside between here and Indy in cocktail weenie-sized pieces. That'd be karma coming home to roost given how many times I've dumped bits and pieces along State Road 37.

What's a matter, you wimp? This doesn't sound like a very nice bedtime story? Well, it ain't. But there are the occasional side-benefits. The perks. I'm talking babes. Serious babes. Why, back in February of 1991, there was this one case—Jesus, Buckley! Stop droolin'!

One: Cracking The Shell

I knew it was going to be a lousy day as soon as I woke up on that ugly Tuesday morning. Most nights, when I'm deep into bottom shelf hooch? I wish I'd never regained consciousness.

Someone had glued shut my eyes with what turned out to be liverwurst. Once I could finally see again, I noticed at least two dozen empty airline bottles of DeKuyper's Crème de Menthe festooning my nightstand. My red satin sheets stuck to my legs as I tried to get out of bed, but I was trapped in a gummy cement of Dusseldorf mustard, Braunschweiger, Maatjes herring in cream sauce, KY Jelly and congealed spooge. I'd like to tell you the previous night had marked a new low even for me, but this scene was kid stuff compared to how I snared the Goat-girl of Guadalupe.

I waited for the room to stop rotating. My skull throbbed as if a den of rutting stoats was trapped within its reconstructed confines. My mouth tasted like the floor of a slaughterhouse. Not ideal, but probably survivable.

I extricated myself from the rank bedclothes and hobbled into the bathroom. The shower curtain was plastered with rapidly spoiling leaves of lox and prosciutto. I squinted at a Post-it Note stuck to the mirror and circled in gaudy teal lipstick. "If you make it out alive, email me where you got the dick implant because Daddy's looking for that kind of gear and I wouldn't mind riding it again either." She'd signed it Deanna and included a phone number. I needed to save her info—Valentine's Day was right around the corner.

Then I power-barfed a five minute torrent of green mung. My cleaning service should be happy that at least half the mess hit the toilet this time. I really needed to write them a long, heartfelt apology.

After I grabbed a cold shower, I searched my medicine cabinet for a preemptive dose of antibiotics. A furry pair of penicillin tabs wrapped in a threadbare g-string would have to do. Chased them with some Pepto. Gritted my teeth to keep everything down. Started a pot of coffee and tried to piece together how this epic stupidity had unfolded.

11

The sheer quantity of my favorite deli treats meant I'd recently hit the jackpot because I scrape by most days on Armour Potted Meat, ramen, and a gallon or so of joe. Plus the cheapest 80 proof I can scrounge at the liquor store conveniently located three blocks from my office. When I opened the fridge to see if there was anything left over from last night's food orgy, I found my trousers and shoes. Stuffed inside my right front pants pocket was a receipt for payment of two grand from my neighborhood shyster. I searched in vain for a deposit slip from my bank; I was in arrears on rent for both my apartment and office as well as my secretary's salary. I prayed I hadn't blown the boodle on debauchery.

Caffeine resurrected memories I would've preferred remain suppressed. After collecting my fee for getting evidence on the owner of a franchise restaurant who was pulling a Chuck Berry with video cams in the women's restroom, I'd hit my bank over on Kirkwood and then dropped into my favorite dive across the street to celebrate with some liquid lunch. And dinner. Jonesing for deli dessert, I teetered up Walnut to Faris Meat Market, which is just downstairs from my apartment. That's where I bought all the cured goodies. I stepped outside and caught a whiff of pizza from Johnny Rockit's up half a block. A group of geeky college kids, which turned out to be the IU chapter of the Star Trek Next Generation Fan Club, was just dispersing. I must've asked this woman who was dressed up as Counselor Troi to name her poison. She turned out to be the club's treasurer and her drink of choice was mint-flavored disinhibitor. The last thing I recalled was her squealing at me to arm my photon torpedoes. Then it was lights out. Yeah, a couple of days of R & R and I'd be ready to nibble on her roddenberries again.

After I gulped down as much coffee as my abused stomach could handle, I put on my cleanest professional clown costume, locked up the apartment, walked down to the second-floor landing, and stole somebody's Indianapolis Star. I was relieved to read that Bush was putting off shipping ground forces into his own private crusade on behalf of the Kuwaiti royal family. Bad news was Iraq had upped the ante by hurling two Scud missiles into Israel. Fourteen years since leaving the public sector and not a single regret.

The temperature had dropped back down to freezing overnight but I couldn't find my trench coat in the apartment. I grabbed my lapels with one hand against the wind and did a dog-trot across the courthouse square. When I went searching for apartments a year ago, I hadn't aimed on getting a place so close to the office. I was far more interested in finding something within staggering distance of the bars that hadn't 86'ed me.

"Another rough night, Ozzie?" murmured my secretary, Angie Rodell, as I nearly fell into the office. She didn't even have to take her eyes off the latest issue of Pudding Pop Confidential to tell what kind of shape I was in. She could smell me sweating out mentholated alcohol and smoked meats through my burnt umber leisure suit.

I'd hired Angie a little over four years ago when business was still booming. She'd majored in primary school education but switched over to accounting after the kindergarten teacher she'd been shadowing slit her wrists in the middle of class, and all the panicked children trampled Angie charging for the door. I needed someone to keep the books and be the smiling face greeting new customers as they walked in the door. This cute, freckled, strawberry blonde from southern Indiana fit the bill. Angie's family raised hogs, and she was a powerfully-built woman more than capable of hoisting a dead pig, drawing, and butchering the animal.

I managed to balance my corpse on the edge of her desk without rolling off. "Look who's talking, kiddo," I archly replied, flicking the oversized alligator clip dangling from her left ear lobe. "Go another round with the high school A.V. club?" A cold draft blew down from the cracked skylight overhead and caught the gauzy fabric of her low-cut blouse. I suddenly got an inexplicable yen for bing cherries.

"Don't ever hit on the support staff, you horny little weasel," I could still hear my mentor at Langley saying when he caught me eyeing a comely receptionist. "You don't want anyone here knowing they got you by your short 'n curlies," Frank Knight had added with a grin. Easy for Frank, I thought. Beautiful wife and twin boys at home.

I had no idea I could still make Angie blush. She plucked off the alligator clip, dropped it in her purse, and said, "Why don't we both try to be professionals for a change, Oz? I've got a client cooling her heels in your office." She tilted her head at the steel-reinforced door behind her desk.

"Will wonders ever cease? Maybe both your paycheck and the rent won't bounce this Friday."

An expression that could have been either annoyance or bran muffin-induced gas crossed Angie's face. "You swore to me you were going to deposit Crossman's check when you left here yesterday morning! I have car payments, rent of my own, I gotta eat and—"

"And send what's left home so the bank don't foreclose on the family farm," I finished her worn-out refrain. "I'm good for it, Angie." I smoothed back the few remaining strands of black hair over the tattoo of Nietzsche on the crown of my head. I recoiled in distaste at the globs of Vicks Vapo-rub adhering to my fingers.

"She must've been one sick puppy," Angie said. I tried to clean off my hands on her blotter pad. "Jesus, don't do that!"

"Right," I said, "we're being professional today." I leaned in and whispered, "So, what's her story?"

Angie chucked the blotter in her trash can. "She wouldn't tell me. Just said her name was Elizabeth Lungs and then something about how you were the only person in Bloomington who could help her now."

"And has she got 'em?"

Angie stared at me. "Huh?"

"Lungs, kiddo. She got the lungs?" I grinned.

"You got a one-track mind, you male chauvinist pig! It's assholes like you that keep us women down!"

"Gotta keep you down, babes. You always wanna be on top," I snickered.

[KB: at this point in our conversation, I embarked on an earnest protest against Osborne's rampant sexism, an outburst he ended by pointing a Glock at my groin and reminding me of the five hundred reasons I was chronicling his detestable capers. Common sense prevailed.]

Angie picked up a pair of bronzed Jersey Red testicles and aimed them at my head, but she must've remembered I never paid her until Fridays. "If you hadn't saved me from the Goat-girl of Guadalupe ..." she muttered.

"And took a slug with your name on it to boot. What's your read on her, Ang? Give me something."

Angie tilted back in her chair and easily tossed the metal boar's nuts from one hand to the other. New priority: get square with the secretary before she bronzes yours. "A lot of poise, but I wouldn't put her past 25. Comes from serious money, Ozzie, dressed like something out of Vogue. Like, Chicago Miracle Mile or New York? Someone might have knocked her around, boss. She's wearing a lot of foundation to cover a bruise on her forehead. She called for an appointment right after I got into the office. Caller ID said an IU number but looks too young to be faculty. Wealthy grad student?" She batted her eyes at me. "But what do I know, boss? I'm just an underpaid little farm girl."

"Christ, you're a goddamn shark, Angie. Which is why I hired you." I adjusted my bolo tie and opened the door to my office. Thanks, babe, I mouthed at her. Fuck you, she silently replied.

Elizabeth Lungs stood behind my desk in profile to me. First impression was graceful, high cheekbones, full lips, and a gym-sculpted physique. She appeared to be staring out my grimy window overlooking College Street. The sun had peeked through a gap between the courthouse's rotunda and a wall of threatening gray clouds. Paper had said snow by Thursday. Elizabeth's head and shoulders were surrounded in a brief halo of light. A perfect angel, I said to myself.

Didn't realize then she was the angel of death.

She must've seen something on the street below she didn't like. Her right arm shot out, and she snatched at the pull cord dangling from the overhead rod. The Venetian blinds rocketed down with an explosion of dust bunnies as big as Airedales. Miss Lungs quickly grabbed her nose. She pivoted to face me, her eyes crossing and uncrossing as a rivulet of bright red blood trickled through her fingers.

"Holy shit!" I cried. "We can take that off your fee, no problem!" Which would be at least double my usual, I estimated, taking in her expensive apparel. Angie's assessment was spot on.

I clumsily brushed the debris off of her back. A blue and gold paisley scarf neatly wrapped her straight, jet black hair. I guessed the scarf cost more than the Colt under my left arm. The scarf matched her knee-length silk dress. She wore a wide royal blue belt on her narrow waist, and her high heels were the same shade as the belt. Perfectly accessorized, I thought. How long did it take her to find the right color shoes, I wondered. And where did she pick up that knot on her noggin?

"My apologies, Miss Lungs. I usually don't have to maim my clients until after I've handed them the bill."

"I was told you hold your sense of humor in high esteem," she said, her rich alto muffled as she tried to staunch her bloody nose. She reached down to one of my client chairs for her royal blue purse. Did she have an entire wardrobe of coordinated purses, shoes, and belts? Triple my fee. She plucked out a wad of tissues. Hot damn! Royal blue kleenex, too!

"I suppose you think you're some sort of comedian."

"By day, yeah, that's me. By night I'm a sex machine."

"Thank God it's still morning," she answered without the hint of a smile. This could get grim fast.

We each did a half turn around my desk. She plopped down in the Naugahyde BarcaLounger opposite from me. I lowered myself into my grandfather's old oak swivel chair. Satisfied that she'd quelled her nosebleed, she tucked her soiled hankies between the cushions of the lounger and leaned forward. Her large, pensive brown eyes began dissecting my face. I waited as she traveled across my shoulders and down my chest.

I'm used to new customers vamping awhile, but this raging hangover was eating away at my manners. "You want me to stand up and drop my trousers?" I asked. "That way, you can get the full effect."

"I think I'm wasting my time," she said. She didn't reach for her purse, though.

"Well, you're certainly wasting mine."

She shook her head. "You aren't what I expected. I don't like your looks."

"Neither do I, Miss Lungs. But then, most things in life don't bear close examination."

"You simply don't look like a man who can be trusted no matter how bad it got. Somebody told me that you were that kind of man. A man who could be trusted."

"Somebody must not know me very well," I tried to laugh.

She made with this lovely little shiver. Her tailor should've suggested the shoulder pads on her dress were overkill, given her

16

athletic frame. Maybe a swimmer? I wanted to see a lot more of what was going on beneath the fabric. "Rico told me you were an honest guy."

I cocked an eyebrow. "Rick Saffire? The bartender? He said that about me? Then why doesn't the bastard ever let me run up a tab?"

She sat up straight in the lounger, wrinkling her nose as if she'd gotten a whiff of my fourth wife's sweat socks. "Give me one good reason I should tell you my problems, Mr. Yesterday."

I hung onto the arms of my desk and suppressed a solid DeKuyper's belch. "Because you got no one else who'll listen, Miss Lungs. Because you told Rico enough for him to agree that going to the cops is not a good move. Rico knows the difference between cop-trouble, lawyer-trouble, and my brand of trouble."

"And what is your brand of trouble, Mr. Yesterday?" she asked. I liked that tremor of uncertainty in the back of her throat. She'd come to the end of her pretend bravado and none too soon. Nobody else had booked an appointment for the day, but if I didn't get some hair of the dog by lunchtime, I might start crying.

I folded my hands over my tormented bowels. "The stuff the rest of those jerks are afraid to touch. The shade of gray that begins to border on black." I gave her the thousand-yard stare that usually gets even the hard cases spoiling their dry-goods. "But I know where the line is, Miss Lungs. I may bend the rules to the breaking point, but I don't cross the line. And I know how to bring a client back over that line." I scrutinized the BarcaLounger. No puddle yet. Was I slipping?

"You wander over the line, Miss Lungs? Is that your problem?"

The back of her hand flew to her forehead. I honestly thought she was going to pass out on me. "I-I-I d-don't think so," she stammered. Her eyelids fluttered, sending little bits of royal blue mascara down her bruised nose.

Quadruple my fee!

"But I am trying to help somebody who has," she managed to say.

"You're looking awfully pale." I got up from my chair and started to head for the door. "You want me to ask my secretary to get you some water?"

"It's my father," she murmured, ignoring the offer. "My father and a man called Pecorino."

That brought the fun and games to a standstill. I slumped back down into my chair. "Which Pecorino?" I managed to say without shitting myself. "There's several guys in town with that name."

"I believe my father said he goes by Peter."

Now it was my turn to get the shakes. "Petey Pecorino?" I said. What was a classy kid like Elizabeth Lungs doing with Slimeball Hall of Famer Petey the Pecker?

My right amygdala jumped so hard that the caudate nucleus pinched shut, momentarily depriving me of all motivational salience. A vast existential chasm of only a few seconds' duration, but long enough for the abyss to stare back at me and make wisecracks about my height.

The Pecker was back in circulation? That meant only one thing and it was my worst nightmare. Why was this happening in February when my favorite drive-in theater was closed? God knows where my back-up was playing snowbird this winter.

Elizabeth's troubles were bigger than I had ever imagined. Much bigger than her nicely ballooned lungs. Which I still wanted to get to know better. Screw the fee. If it wasn't for Angie's salary, I'd do this gig pro bono to get a shot at bringing down that fat fuck, Petey.

"You've come to the right man, Miss Lungs. Let's take it from the top."

She nodded slowly, then bent over to clutch at her shapely knees. "That's what Rico told me you would say," she said. She lifted her eyes up, tears running down her cheeks. "Tell me, Mr. Yesterday, what do you know about dinosaur eggs?"

Two: The Yolk's On Me

"Dinosaur eggs?" I repeated. "Petey the Pecker is involved with dinosaur eggs?" The Pecker? A man who couldn't tell a souffle from a mound of wombat vomit? Okay, so for that matter, neither could I.

"I'd better start from the beginning," Miss Lungs said. "My grandfather was a member of the American Museum of Natural History's expedition that discovered a clutch of dinosaur eggs in the Gobi Desert in the 1920s. Grandpa was the person who unearthed the protoceratops eggs, but the Museum shortchanged him on his expenses. He was afraid he'd get no credit for his work." She took another tissue out of her purse and dabbed at her eyes. "This is an old family skeleton, Mr. Yesterday. I can't possibly go to the authorities.

"Grandpa got greedy and kept one of the eggs for himself. Before he died, he gave the egg to my father. We lived in Indianapolis while I was growing up. Daddy owned a medical supply manufacturing plant. All it made in the beginning was colostomy bags. We did well at first." Her chin began quivering. "A few years ago, just as I was starting college, some bigger companies undercut Daddy. The business started going under. Daddy wanted to switch over to, um, prophylactics, because of the AIDS epidemic, but he needed money fast. Quite a lot of money. To convert the plant's operations, you know? But he couldn't convince the banks to give him a conventional business loan, so—"

"So he went to Petey the Pecker, a highly successful drug-dealer, who has a reputation for laundering dirty money with very clean investments," I deduced. Colostomy king turns to drug lord to break into the rubber game. How many more times was it going to happen?

"Here's how this works, Miss Lungs. Your father quickly learns he's got the same problem with condoms that he had with colostomy bags. He can't compete with the big boys like Trojan. The business slides even deeper into the red. Your father can't keep up on the vig, the interest Petey's demanding. So ol' Pecorino starts scoping out every source of collateral. Say ...this dino egg?" Nicely done, I thought, congratulating myself. "Exactly how much is a dinosaur egg worth these days?"

"This one? From what Daddy told me, it would probably cover his entire debt, if this Pecorino crook knew the right buyer." Elizabeth Lung's lithe body shook with a marvelous shudder of despair. "That's only half the story, though, Mr. Yesterday," she said in a hopeless voice. "The business went under because Daddy bought some defective machinery. A lot of the thingies, the prophylactics. They had tiny holes in them. Daddy's lawyer told him we could probably duck the product liability suits. But the leaky condoms made Mr. Pecorino mad, Mr. Yesterday. Do you know how else condoms can be used?"

Pecorino. Drugs. Scumbags. Punctured scumbags, at that. Yeah, I knew how drug dealers used rubbers. Mules smuggling drugs over the border or through Customs packed condoms with coke and H, then swallowed them or shoved them up where the sun don't shine. Leaky rubbers equaled some dead mules and a lot more lost merchandise. Which all added up to one pissed-off Pecker, especially when you factored in Petey working for the most bloodthirsty motherfucker I'd ever encountered.

"You said your father could be in trouble. Did he supply a bunch of free rubbers to Pecorino, knowing how they'd be used?"

She shook her head emphatically. "Daddy was completely ignorant of the drug smuggling until Pecorino heard about the lawsuits. Then Pecorino threatened him and Daddy just ... just vanished!" The kid finally broke down, a series of forlorn sobs wracking her toothsome bod. She held up her hand as I rose once more to call for Angie.

"No," she said, "I'm all right. Daddy's in hiding. Somewhere. I'm not sure where. He's afraid to go to the police. I'm afraid! He thinks he'll be named as a, what was it? As a co-conspirator! If Pecorino gets arrested! And then, somehow, Pecorino found out about the egg, Mr. Yesterday! About how valuable it is!" Her red-rimmed eyes slowly met my sympathetic gaze. "He came to the house last Friday night. He hit me with a gun. He knocked me senseless, and then he made me show him where the egg was. He stole the egg, and now he says he's going to kill me unless I meet him tonight and tell him where Daddy's staying!" She teared up again and cried, "I can't go! Don't you see,

Mr. Yesterday—he'll kill me because I don't have any idea where Daddy is!"

She doubled over, all that panic and fear crushing the tough little girl act she'd put on minutes ago. I've got a real soft spot for scared, crying women. Especially when they're in their early twenties and built for mischief.

I squatted down and hugged Elizabeth Lungs. My careless fingers gently brushed her heaving Torquemadas. (Try not to get too excited, okay, Buckley?) The scents of expensive French soap and lotus flower adorned her hair. Mine still reeked of carnal excess. Did I need to start using something stronger than Ivory?

A plan coalesced in the camphorated recesses of my brain.

I grasped her shoulders and pushed her away from me. "You're right, Miss Lungs," I said. "You can't meet Pecorino. He's far too dangerous. Where and when are you supposed to connect with the Pecker tonight?"

Her body was still shaking, but she managed to sputter, "Eleven o'clock, at Lower Cascades Park. By the big shelter."

Perfect, I thought. Poor lighting and the sky would be blacker than the backs of my teeth if this storm kept rolling in. "I'll have to borrow your car, Miss Lungs. Manual or automatic transmission?"

She blinked at me, then said it was an automatic. "I wouldn't think that mattered to a resourceful man like you, Mr. Yesterday."

I patted her cheek, inadvertently smearing her prominent maxillary process with a little Vicks. "I'll be waiting out of sight in the shelter. My secretary will be the one driving your car and she prefers a stick." The underpaid little farm girl.

"Your secretary? Isn't that too risky?"

"You leave that to me, Miss Lungs. Angie will be happy to do the job." Almost as happy as she'd be going back to my place and cleaning up after me and Counselor Troi, I ruefully thought. I returned to my desk and pulled a standard contract out of my lap drawer. "You said yourself you can't go. I plan to get the drop on Petey before he's close enough to your car to see it isn't you."

"So you'll take my case?" she softly asked. "You'll help me?"

I flashed her my most reassuring smile, although the effort nearly broke my jaw. "I took your case as soon as you mentioned Pecorino." Shaking that punk down will be the first fun I've had since Tammy

Faye Bakker left a couple pounds of rouge on my thighs, I wanted to tell her, but she didn't seem in the mood for that horrible story.

Elizabeth Lungs scribbled her signature on the VapoRub-stained document. She reached in her purse without a moment's hesitation, extracted a matching clutch, and produced a sheaf of crisp Franklins. "Will this cover tonight?" she smiled.

I tried my best not to jump up and down like a giddy school girl and said, "Quite nicely," as if accepting thousand dollar retainers was an everyday occurrence. I asked for her address and instructed her that Angie and I would be there at nine o'clock sharp so I could make sure we were all on the same page.

My new client primped a bit with a compact mirror to make herself as presentable as possible. She thanked me profusely on the way through the reception area and allowed me to escort her all the way down the hall to the elevator. We parted with a handshake, but I expected Miss Lungs would find some more mutually satisfactory manner of expressing her gratitude once I squashed the Pecker.

When I got back to the office, I reclined across Angie's desk and grinned broadly at her. "How would you like some real excitement tonight, kiddo?" I said. "No alligator clips involved. Unless you beg me."

Her eyes narrowed, and she looked up at me over the top of her gold-chased glasses. "Why do I get the feeling that I'll wish you were gonna proposition me instead of this excitement?" she whined.

I straightened up and slid two of the benjamins her way. "One of my favorite goons is trying to shake down the lovely Miss Lungs, Ang. He's demanded a meeting at 11 tonight. You and I are going to head over to Elizabeth's place two hours beforehand, and then you're going to drive to the meet disguised as our client."

Angie studied the cash then scowled up at me. "I don't know, Ozzie. She's got that straight black hair I'd kill for and I'm stuck with this curly rat's nest."

"No sweat," I said. "I got a wig that's perfect for this job."

She guffawed. "The topless shoeshine schtick?"

"Professional all the way in this office, kiddo."

She wedged the hundreds down her ample frontage. "Two conditions, boss," she said. "My salary in cash tomorrow, and I go to this thing armed."

"Deal," I said, bidding a wistful goodbye to the three pitchers of martinis I was going to boil my brain in at some after-hours joint once I'd finished rearranging the Pecker's face. "Your carry license still good?"

"All up to date." She drained her coffee mug. "And Oz? Hook me up with some stopping power this time. That pearl-handled Raven .25 you loaned me might be fine for Nancy Reagan, but I want genuine heat."

"A .25 would only piss off this asshole, Angie. We'll get you a nice hand cannon for tonight." I turned her desk clock around to face me. "I gotta make some calls, Ang. Since this is gonna be a long night, why don't you knock off for the day? I'll pick you up here at, what, 8:30?"

"Sounds like a plan, Ozzie," she said. "Just remember to lock everything down. And for the love of Christ, no booze until this is over, okay?"

"Aye, aye," I said, saluting her.

Good thing she only said booze, I thought as I listened to her pumps click down the hall. I bolted the outer door, returned to my office, and opened the bottom drawer of my filing cabinet.

Voila! My trench coat! Under my coat was a stack of German porn, and beneath the porn lay a plastic envelope of pharmaceutical-grade Colombian flake. I never have to go out of my way looking for contraband; substances come searching for me. I'd accepted this plump bindle of dancing dust by way of payment from a dishy little ginger hooker who was getting manhandled by some bully who thought she needed a pimp. Sure, I'd told Miss Lungs I stayed on my side of the line, but I'm kinda vague on where several victimless offenses fall.

I sat down at my desk for a dainty and thoroughly professional toot. Just to clear away the last remaining traces of Crème de Menthe, you dig? Lightning with a chase of delicious numbness shot up my left nostril. "Mama!" I whimpered. I'd almost forgotten what it felt like to be a god. Every surface and outline in my office sparkled even though I hadn't dusted in a month. I momentarily wondered if it was too soon to call back that nubile young Trek nerd.

C'mon, you poon hound, I told myself, strictly business until you've pounded some Pecker. "That didn't sound too perverted, did it?" I asked my Rolodex. I flipped cards until I found the embossed job for Seriously Weird Solutions. No address, no names, only a toll-free number with a prerecorded message on the other end asking me to punch in my number. I did so, hung up, and drummed my fingers in coke-fueled agitation for almost a quarter of an hour before my phone rang. Thank the Lord. I almost started cleaning the windows. I don't do windows. Or cleaning.

"Osborne Yesterday, private investigator," I yelped.

"Jesus H. Christ in a ball cap," replied the familiar redneck twang. "You set your pants on fire again, son?"

"Bite me, Gunga," I said. I counted to one hundred by sevens in my head, trying to put the brakes on my accelerating limbic system. That took all of two seconds. "How fast can you make it to Bloomington from where you are?" I gabbled.

"Not as fast as the crap you've snorted," he laughed. "Does someone need another visit to Betty Ford?"

"You lied about that shithole. There was no bottle service."

"But you loved the coffee enemas. Admit it, guy."

I was usually good for at least half an hour of clowning around with my fellow former CIA special analyst, Jimmy Dale Phemister, but I was revved and ready for lift-off. "Bloomington. Tonight, Gunga. Can you do it?" I said through grinding teeth. "I am going toe to toe with one Petey Pecorino at 11 in the p.m., and I need reinforcements."

I heard him exhale the word "shit" in at least four syllables. "Is the Devil behind this?" Gunga asked, instantly out of jokes. "Is he finally coming after you?"

We didn't mention the Devil's real name over the phone. Even on a secure line. Not since the clusterfuck in Thailand. Not for the last twenty-three years.

"The Pecker's putting the screws to a new client," I explained. "Brand new. He's got no idea I'm involved or that I'm going to come down on him. Like a ton of bricks. Feet first. Brass knuckles. Aluminum ball bat. K-bar. My service Colt. Sawed-off 12 gauge under my car seat. A rocket launcher if I could score it. Locked and loaded."

"But you don't want to take any chances," Gunga said. Statement, not a question.

"My client's easy pickings for someone like Pecorino, but no," I said. Why the hell else would I be calling? I wanted to scream. Okay, so I wasn't going to do a second bump. Probably. "You and I both know Petey's a chickenshit punk, but he might bring extra muscle to the dance."

I could almost hear Gunga tugging on his mustache. "Will we be enough? You wanna bring in Frank's kid just in case?"

"Not for an extrajudicial beat-down," I said. "But I'll be happy to give Knight the collar after we're finished with this prick." Angie with a Sig Sauer, Gunga and I armed to the teeth? Better than a platoon from Special Forces. "We're good."

Jim paused again. I wondered if I'd lost the connection. "Give me a few to rustle up transport," he said. "Can you sit tight at this number without your head exploding?"

I did my best to convince him I was just eager to stomp Petey and hung up. Then I rearranged the furniture. After that, I perused color samples Angie had picked up from Sherwin-Williams. Tavern Taupe! We'd paint the office Tavern Taupe. Adored the name. Tonight I could skin Pecorino and save money on a drop cloth.

I only had to climb the walls another ten minutes before Gunga called back. "A friend of a friend I did a favor for is setting me up on a business partner's private jet, but the pilot won't fly into your Podunk airport, son. He can have me at Indy sometime between 8:30 and 9. Will that work?"

I would've preferred that he be at Elizabeth Lungs' place for the planning session, but I'd take what I could get on such short notice. I told him I'd have Classy Chassis, the limo service we always used, waiting for him, and that I'd send notes and Polaroids of the park with the driver. We hung up, and I dug through my closet for the camera. I needed to scoot if I was going to shoot strategic perches in the park, write out the details, and deliver the package to Classy Chassis, but I was cooking with gas now. What could go wrong?

Okay, scratch that. Plenty could go wrong.

Our client, Angie, and I met, did our homework, and then Miss Lungs hid in the back seat of my car as I drove in circles before installing her in a room at my favorite no-tell motel. Angie drove Elizabeth's car, which was the only vehicle in the parking lot of Lower

Cascades Park. I was hunkered down twenty yards away from Ang, pressed against the shelter's rough-hewn limestone chimney and completely hidden in the shadows.

The park was dead. Didn't feel right.

I checked the luminous dial of my wristwatch. Two minutes to go, and not a sign of Petey. I was beginning to worry that he might've staked out Elizabeth's place on Prow Avenue, possibly figuring he'd been deked. I also wondered if I'd fucked up and failed to notice Pecorino sneaking up through the woods behind me. After the call I'd made to Jim, however, I was sure I'd protected my backside. There was a thick carpet of half-frozen leaves and twigs in the forest, but no one would hear Gunga swooping in.

I was starting to sweat blood just as I spied a pair of headlights bouncing down the road towards the shelter. I immediately recognized the pattern of the car's low beams. A vintage Datsun 510. Drove one of those all over the Alleghenies tracking migratory birds packed with tiny capsules of 3-quinuclidinyl benzilate. The Datsun wasn't exactly Petey's speed, but the junker was almost certainly boosted. Probably stolen plates, too.

Pecorino circled the parking lot, sweeping the shelter house and Elizabeth's Volvo with his lights. I hoped the wig had him fooled. He stopped at the walkway to the shelter house, midway between Angie and where I was crouching. I had a perfect line of vision. This was going to be a cakewalk.

I trained the barrel of my Colt on the Pecker's heap. He didn't seem inclined to get out of his car, and that bothered me. He was acting way too cagey for the impulsive creep I knew. Why didn't he take cover in the shelter or behind a tree to wait for his prey?

I really needed him to make a move. I wouldn't have any trouble blowing away the Pecker if he showed the first sign of going in heavy, but it would be tough explaining matters to the cops in the unlikely event he'd come unarmed. I prayed Angie stuck to our plan and stayed in the Volvo without flashing the inside lights. That wig would only get us so far.

The driver of the Datsun finally got antsy and opened his door. I knew something was wrong as soon as he twisted out of the car. Petey Pecorino was a sawed-off tank of a guy, maybe even a couple inches shorter than me. The guy standing beside the Datsun was tall and

26

lanky, easily six feet, with a heavy beard. Didn't feel like any of the Pecker's known associates, either. Something about him screamed IU student to me.

He bent over to retrieve a large box from the passenger's seat and started walking towards Angie.

I brought my pistol up, yelling at him to freeze. He spun in place, juggling the box. It dropped to the pavement and I heard a sound like a ceramic pot breaking. Then I heard a far worse noise. It was the sound of your proverbial heavy, blunt instrument intersecting with the back of my skull. I'm guessing this was followed by the sound of my face smashing into the concrete floor of the shelter, but I wasn't around to hear that shit.

Three: Keep Your Sunny-Side To Yourself

At first, I thought I'd been subjected to another one of my partner's sadistic practical jokes. Who else besides Gunga Jim would've dropped an alcohol-soaked rhino on my head? Then I started worrying about all the delicate surgery that various poorly reimbursed VA croakers had performed on me. My cranium was little more than a jumble of bones held together with gel foam, steel plates, stove bolts, and possibly wads of duct tape. My cerebellum was connected to my medulla oblongata with three chrome brads, and all that kept my third ventricle from wobbling out of my ears was an epoxy shaft sunk into my peduncle.

I tried opening my eyes. The riot of colors and shapes made no sense. Had the blow to my head driven my occipital lobe all the way through my Sylvian fissure? And what of my temporal lobe? I was deaf in my right ear, and it sounded as if a syphilitic mariachi band was playing Edgard Varèse's Ionisation in my left.

The ungodly cacophony mutated into rhythmic machine noises and the nasal voice of my own physician, Melvin Fesance, saying, "Aw, shit! His vitals are stabilizing. And I thought I'd make a few bucks off the boys from the med school!"

"You could detonate a pound of C4 in Ozzie's nose without doing any damage," replied an equally pitiless asshole.

I opened my throbbing eyes to a stream of harsh fluorescent light. The repellant mug of one Deputy Sheriff Robert X. Slorby settled in front of me like a sad bowel movement.

"Sorry to disappoint both of you jerks," I groaned. "Takes a lot more than a crack on the coconut to stop me." I gripped the sides of the gurney and flexed my arms.

Dr. Fesance sprang forward to restrain me. "I wouldn't try sitting up if I were you, Osborne," he warned.

"Why not?" I wriggled free, sat up in a single fluid motion, and opened my mouth in astonishment as a cataract of last evening's three Big Macs hit Slorby square in the chest.

"Projectile vomiting," the doctor chirped. "Quite common in cases of severe concussion."

"Gee, thanks, peeper," Slorby said in a gruff deadpan. "I was gettin' kinda cold here." He turned towards a pale, trembling nurse. She was trying to back-pedal out of the examination room. "Before you start blowin' chunks too, honey, could ya get me a fuckin' towel?" he bellowed. The nurse scampered off to the Emergency Room desk, making guttural noises.

"You sure have a way with dames, Deppity Bob," I tried to laugh. My brains might still be scrambled, but I remembered how much Slorby hated the nickname. The previously spotless white room was spinning in tight circles. I focused on a glob of that special sandwich sauce dangling from Bob's left chest pocket and managed to slow the riotous movement to a crawl.

"Oh yeah?" Slorby sneered, wiping his hands on Doc Fesance's white lab coat. "And you have a nasty habit of leaving ventilated corpses lying all over the landscape." He wheeled on Fesance and bawled, "Don't you have something else you should be doing? Like signing this bastard's release forms?"

"I don't think Mr. Yesterday is going anywhere today," Mel retorted. "He's suffered a significant head trauma. I want to schedule him for more thorough imaging before he goes home. Why, he might even be hemorrhaging—"

"Whatever's happened to his head ain't gonna begin to compare to the significant trauma I'm gonna give you when I hang your balls around your neck like a damn stethoscope!" Slorby shouted. "Release this idiot to my care and get the hell outa here!"

Fesance got up in Bob's doughy face. "Don't fuck with me, Deputy, or I won't look the other way the next time you bring in a prisoner you and your brown-shirted gorillas have stomped."

I wanted to applaud, but all I could do was offer Mel a feeble wave. "Go grab some air, Doc," I said. "I need to get up to speed on this corpse business."

Bob and the doctor engaged in another protracted alpha male staring contest. Mel reluctantly left the room in a cloud of testosterone.

"You know what I like about you, Slorby?" I grinned. "You're so incredibly tactful."

Deppity Bob stabbed my hospital gown with a pink sausage of a finger. "And you are under arrest, Yesterday!"

"Arrest? For what? Falling out of a tree in the park?"

"Falling out of a tree, is it?" He'd opened the closet where my clothes were hanging and hurled my shirt and pants at me. They smelled like someone had soaked them in cheap bourbon. What the hell?

"Yeah, sure. I dreamed I was a chimp climbing in a tree. Or was I really a chimp dreaming I was Osborne Yesterday climbing a tree? A Taoist paradox, don't you think?" I probably needed to take this a little more seriously.

"I'll give you a paradox right up the butt, Yesterday!" he squawked. "I got one dead man, with a .45 sized-hole through his heart and a cartridge from your recently fired gun lodged in the dashboard of his car!"

"Tell me another," I said. I swatted away my clothes. Then I remembered the tall bearded guy in the jalopy with a box. I raised my head without puking and frowned at Slorby. "What else did you find?"

"A Datsun 510, your pile of crap behind the shelter house, some tire tracks and a metal carton full of smashed rock," Bob rasped. He smiled wickedly. "'Course, I've already Mirandized you, and you've waived your rights, hear? The doctor's my witness."

"Hung up on procedure," I said. "Typical anal-retentive."

"I've retained an anus, all right. Your ass is mine, Yesterday."

My mind was in no condition for heavy lifting, but if I didn't wiggle out of this goat-rope pronto, Bob would haul me away in cuffs. I had no doubts about the reception awaiting me in county lock-up.

"How did you find out about the shooting?"

"Got an anonymous tip from someone jogging through the park," he said without checking any notes.

"When?"

"Why does that matter to you, shit bird?" he angrily said, but he did pull a small spiral notebook out of his back pocket. "Dispatch said 11:15 p.m.."

"I didn't get beaned until shortly after 11 and the park was empty." He made with a derisive snort. "Bob, this is a freakin' set-up. How does it make sense that I shoot someone and then drop in my tracks with the back of my skull stove in? I sapped myself? Neat fucking trick."

"You're a derelict wet brain who's one black-out drunk away from the DTs," Slorby fired back. "You went to pull the victim's plug last night drunk as a skunk, got off a lucky shot, and then passed out. Banged your head on the shelter floor where we found you. Hell, I can still smell the booze on you!"

"The only reason you can smell liquor is because the goon who bashed me poured a pint of Four Roses on me after I was down for the count," I said. "Feel my shirt—it's still wet. I have the greatest respect for Kentucky bonded. I only take it internally, Bob." He scoffed at me, so I asked, "Did anyone check my blood alcohol when they brought me in?"

When he didn't answer that one, I folded my arms across my chest and leaned back against the pillow. "The clown who hit me wasn't even smart enough to bring a flexible necked funnel and pour it down my gullet after he clocked me. Get real, Bob. I'm not a shooter. Hits aren't my style!" (Well, not anymore.) "I went out to the park last night to meet with a guy who was trying to shake down a client. This fellow who got offed wasn't supposed to be there. I don't know who the hell he was."

Bob's face did something weird. He got a smile bigger than Counselor Troi's when I started smearing her juicy kibble and bits with the Vicks.

Damn. I apparently needed a brain injury to get that back. What other savage horrors lurked beneath? Might be good to know what worked when I drunk-dialed her for a rematch.

Slorby was beaming like an idiot. "That's the real sweet thing, Os-hole. You do know the deceased. One Kyle Fiffie? Guy you roughed up while you were tracking down some, what was it? Stolen genital jewelry?"

Years of training in resistance to interrogation, indoctrination, and exploitation, as the Company called it, kept me from moving a muscle. Fiffie? The demented Professor Wardigus' prize singing gofer! "Bad coincidence," I smiled, tossing my clothes back at him. Anything for a distraction. "Give me a break, Bob! This stinks, and you know it. Why would I publicly wax a guy who filed a battery suit against me?" He shook his head. "Hey—I saved you from the Goat-girl of Guadalupe!"

31

"And took a bullet with my name on it, to boot," he admitted. "But that don't wipe out murder, bozo." He calmly picked his yellowed teeth with his thumbnail. "So, someone was shaking down a client, you say? Well, let's get all our cards on the table. Who was the client?"

I rolled my eyes. "We gotta play this game? That's privileged information. I won't tell you squat without a subpoena from Judge Grange."

"Goddamnit, Yesterday, this is a freaking homicide!" Slorby exploded. "We don't like homicides in B-town, you dumb mother! The client's a suspect, and you're gonna give him to me!"

"In a pig's eye, I will." Speaking of pigs, I thought, I wondered what had happened to my favorite hog castrator. "I will give you the extortionist, though. My guess is he did the shooting."

"You'll give me whatever I want you to give me! I've got your gun and a slug to match smack dab through Fiffie's heart!"

"You also got Petey Pecorino," I answered.

"Petey the Pecker? Bullshit, Yesterday! This ain't his kinda action either!"

"Sorry, Bob, but it looks like Pecorino is involved," interjected a strong baritone from the doorway. There, with a manila folder in his paws, stood my blue-uniformed godson, Bloomington Police Department Lieutenant Detective Neon Knight.

Neon was a square-jawed, clean-shaven and crew cut guy who looked like he'd stepped out of a Wheaties commercial or a Marines recruiting poster. Frank Knight, my mentor and operations commander, had originally christened his son Nelson. The kid couldn't stand the name, so he dropped the middle two letters once he became a rebellious teenager. Hence "Neon." Made for some fine cognitive dissonance, given his appearance. Only a handful of us knew he cultivated the look to disarm and gain acceptance in an intolerant environment.

"There was another set of prints on the gun. Not easy to lift off your contoured grip, Ozzie, but they're Petey's."

"Crap!" said Bob. He leaned against the clothes locker, banging the doors in frustration with both fists. "Just when I think I got this town cleaned out and you in jail, Pecorino blows away my vic."

32

"Can't win 'em all," I chuckled. God, I was playing this stupid. I should've been spilling my guts about the case. The cops had already lifted my prints and run them through the system? Where was Angie, and what happened to Gunga? My head was pounding like Ginger Baker's double kick drums. I wasn't going to find any answers from a hospital bed. I managed to bring the clock over the door into focus. 9:43?

"Look, Bob," I said, "let me get this thing with the client straightened out. I'll call you as soon as I bring him up to speed, and then I'll help you nail Pecorino. I know the Pecker's moves ten times better than you, and he obviously has it in for me. We've got a longstanding beef. Besides, nobody's gonna coldcock me without losing some teeth."

"You can have all the time alone with Petey you want, but you gotta share," Slorby said. "What's all this about the metal carton Fiffie was carrying?"

"Preliminary analysis says some kind of fossilized shell," Neon replied for me. "Shattered into dozens of pieces."

"Pecorino stole a valuable dinosaur egg from my client. He wanted money for it," I decided to reveal.

"How does Fiffie fit in?" Bob persisted. "You got any idea how much heat I am getting from town and gown over a murdered student?"

I shook my head. "Look, Slorby, my client obviously handed me a bunch of horse manure. That's why I want to confront him and get the straight story. Alone. Once I know the connection between him and Pecorino, I'll call you." Him, I thought. Misdirection and obfuscation. And a possible obstruction charge, but business first.

Slorby shoved his bulbous nose in my face. "You do that, Yesterday," he spat. "You make damn sure you call me! I'm givin' you exactly 'til 5 p.m. to get things nice and straight, and then I want answers! I'm doing you a big favor, peeper, 'cause you done me a few over the years. You screw this up? All your CIA buddies won't be able to find where I've buried you. You understand?"

"Loud and clear, Bob. Loud and clear."

Neon politely slid in between us. "I'll keep an eye on Osborne, Robert," he promised. "The Chief also wants to see this resolved as quickly as possible." He put a friendly hand on Deppity Bob's upper arm. "I'll sign him out and drive him back to his car, Sheriff. And have a little heart-to-heart with the stubborn bastard."

Slorby was clearly unhappy with the arrangement, but behaving like a prick wouldn't give him any traction with Neon or BPD. When he'd finally stomped off, Frank's kid picked my clothes up off the floor and gave them to me. "You really fit to leave?" he asked. "You look like shit on a cracker, Oz."

"Trust me, Neon, I've had worse," I grinned. As I wrestled into my damp, mud-streaked threads, I gave him an edited version of the Lungs case. I needed someone trustworthy to hunt Elizabeth's license plate so I could start figuring out where Angie was. "You post a BOLO on Pecorino?"

"Absolutely. Soon as I had the ID."

"And just how did you make the Pecker's prints that quick, son?" I asked on our way to the hospital's central elevators. "Even the feds can't cough up results in less than a day."

"Jim Phemister woke me up at around four in the morning. Said he was supposed to be providing back-up for you last night but hit a snag. He got suspicious when he couldn't reach you and dropped Petey's name." Neon shrugged. "We've never been able to make anything stick on Pecorino, so we regularly haul him in as a person of interest if someone's moving quantity. We got several mint copies of his prints. His right thumb popped on the butt of your piece, just below the trigger guard."

"Thank God that dumb mook didn't think to wear gloves," I said.

Neon glanced at me. "One of the things I don't like about this, Oz. Kind of strange for a guy who's careful enough to avoid prosecution all this time." That was bothering me as well. I wasn't going to complain.

"What about anyone in Pecorino's crowd?" Neon asked me while we walked out to the reserved parking area where he'd left his cruiser. "What else can I do on this? Bob may be a colossal pain in the ass, but he's right about the ruckus Fiffie's murder is causing."

I waited until we were in the car to answer. "Son, I want Petey to fry for this just as bad as Slorpy, but you and I both know who the Pecker's been fronting since I arrived and why he'd take a poke at me." Neon's grip on the wheel tightened, and I noticed a red splotch over his cheekbone.

"If that bastard comes anywhere near Bloomington, I get the first shot at him, Osborne," Neon demanded. "Swear to me, Pops. He fucking blew up my dad."

"Yeah, he did. Dza-lu busted some of my favorite parts as well, son, but you got dibs on his ass as far as I'm concerned." I tried to turn my head without barfing. Maybe Fesance was right and I should stay overnight.

"We all need to be careful, Neon. Dza-lu will kill anything and everyone in his path when he finally comes to finish me off. He'll be looking for you as well, just because Frank was your father." Gunga, too, although I was still pissed that he'd let me down last night. "I don't want to take any chances with you," I told him. "If he's here, let's corner him on our own terms so we can wipe out the monster without any collateral damage."

Neon slowly nodded his head. "I'll keep this as quiet as I can, Ozzie. Just don't fuck this up." He pulled up to the impound lot off Seventh Street. Went into his no-nonsense cop mode and said, "I love you like a father, Oz, but you've been redlining your beat-up hide since Thailand. Slorby wants to hang you from the highest limb, and I can't write off any more DUIs. Do this right and do it sober, okay, Pops?"

I did my best to look contrite. All I could think about was a late breakfast of Screwdrivers and a heaping spoonful of marching powder. Neon accepted my oath that I was sober the previous evening and I had every intention of staying that way until we locked up the Pecker.

We stepped inside the impound office, and Neon cleared the paperwork on my '64 Valiant. I had my keys back in a matter of minutes. I wanted my service piece returned as well, but knew I'd probably seen the last of my old beloved Colt. Should've just been thankful that the towing service hadn't wrenched the Red Baron to scrap.

Mournfully concluding that a few jiggers of Smirnoff on top of a head injury might interfere with the investigation, I headed over to my office instead of the boozerama which stood only two tempting blocks away. The elevator had gone tits up for the third time this month, so I bounded up the two flights of stairs despite my raging headache. As I rushed down the hall, I could already see the office was dark. No Angie. I mentally listed the atrocities I'd perform on Pecorino's miserable carcass. I groped for my keys, and when I threw open the door, I saw the little red light flashing on my answering machine. I thumped the "message" button and sank down into Angie's chair.

"This is Angie, boss." Her southern Indiana drawl was very small and very scared. "I am supposed to tell you they have me and Elizabeth Lungs. They promise to let both of us go once they're sure you've dropped her case. And don't call the police, Ozzie. They want you to sit tight and wait for a call explaining where you can meet Pecorino. They say I'm supposed to tell you that if you don't follow these instructions, you probably won't be able to recognize what's left of either Elizabeth or me." The tape stopped, and that was all there was to it.

I sat there like a pithed animal, blindly gazing at the top of Angie's desk. I barely heard the front door open. When I finally looked up, I was staring down the barrel of a .44 Ruger Super Blackhawk. At least I wouldn't have to worry about this damn headache.

Four: Fried Or Scrambled?

I pressed my glabella up against the Ruger's black triangular sight. "Why don't you just pull the trigger and put me out of your misery, amigo?" I said

Gunga Jim Phemister, former executive commander of Operation Phoenix and now regional field officer for a nameless federal agency, guffawed. Gunga had been a rangy kid with thinning hair when I first met him when we were rookies at Langley in 1964. He purposefully sought out any field assignment providing him an excuse to grow back his mustache, and he often had this Groucho thing going on with his unruly dark hair, horn-rimmed glasses, and caustic sarcasm. In the past few years, he'd put on some padding and traded up for some more fashionable aviator frames, but the mustache and evil wit were permanent fixtures.

He stowed the revolver in his emu leather shoulder holster, dropped a gray gym bag by my desk, and took a chaw out of what I hoped was not a dehydrated jerked ferret. "Got any Everclear around here?" he asked. Should I tell him about the coke?

"If I did, I'd already be lying under this desk," I replied. "Are those fresh sores on your mouth? Have the girls at Gunga's House of A Thousand Torments been getting their shots? And where the hell were you last night?"

Gunga gingerly patted his oozing lower lip. "So much for all your forensics training, kid. Them's bite-marks."

"Been necking with the chickens again?" I cut short one of his patented comebacks. "Answer my question, damnit. I got a lump on the head the size of a gas stove and a corpse down at the morgue 'cause some derelict wasn't watching my back last night!"

My old comrade-in-arms slouched down on the Louis Quinze chaise lounge beside Angie's filing cabinet. Amazing what you can squeeze outta some IU department chair who needs a borderline side piece escorted out of state. "You got a lot more problems besides a cracked skull and a stiff," he said. "Boy, you been holding news conferences about your plans with this Lungs woman, or do you just have your secretary phone your every move to Dza-lu?" Before I had a chance to ask how much Librium he'd swallowed with his morning dose of Air Wick, Gunga told me, "Guy, your security sucks. I was ambushed last night. Ferocious redheaded chick driving that limo you sent me."

I leaned my forehead into my shaking hands. "I specifically asked Rick Saffire's brother to handle this. There's no redheads working at Classy Chassis."

"Yeah, well, I figured that part after she left me lying face down in a cow patty near Waverly," Gunga cheerfully replied. "Too bad I didn't notice Dza-lu's cute little brand on her inner thigh until after I started passing out."

"Then it's your fault, you cretin. You had no business taking a drink before going on surveillance!"

Gunga's scored mouth wrinkled in a wry and vaguely lewd grin. "Did I say anything about a drink? My bet is that she'd mixed some of Dza-lu's secret herbs and spices into her nipple rouge. Or smeared it south of the border, if you catch my drift."

"Spare me the details, okay? So, she was one of the necromancer's b-girls?"

His back arched with an exaggerated Elvis hip-thrust. "No, I'd give her an A-minus. At least!" He sank into the chaise again and put his hands behind his head.

"After I came to and took a very expensive cab ride from Martinsville, I got on the horn with Classy Chassis. They said you canceled my pick-up less than an hour after you dropped off an envelope to give me. Said you'd sent your secretary to pick up your intel. Wanna bet the redhead was playing your secretary?"

I squeezed my eyes shut. "Fuck. Yesterday morning Elizabeth Lungs saw something she didn't like down on the street and snapped my blinds closed. She knew she had a tail on her."

"A tail she could pick up and you didn't?" Gunga said in disbelief. "Boy, you lost your edge?"

"I may have gotten sloppy canvasing the park and checking in with the limo service, but whoever snatched Elizabeth last night must've sicced a team of vehicles on me," I said. I was getting way too defensive. I also needed to check in with the motel where I'd stashed Elizabeth Lungs.

"Does this sound more organized than Petey the Pecker could ever be?"

"We need to follow that line of inquiry somewhere else. Let's go to my car and get some fresh air," I said, catching a sour whiff of jerky-scented methane. Gunga bit down on the last of his mystery meat and followed me to the back stairway.

On the way to my car, I filled him in on Angie, Fiffie, and the shattered dino egg. An iron-gray sky was pissing down fine, icy bullets. I'd tell you February is not Bloomington at its finest, but the weather was pretty uniform shit from November through March. And don't get me started on the humidity in the summer. Made me wish I'd moved out with my father's people in Peridot, Arizona. They didn't want me, though, and I couldn't blame them.

"I'm going to drop you off at Enterprise," I told Gunga. "I want you to drive back up to Indianapolis and check out father Lungs and his dying condom factory."

"What for? They need a live model for their 'big and tall' line?"

"I didn't know sheep were into safe sex," I murmured out of the corner of my mouth. "No, you deviant. I want some deep background on the Lungs family. Something stinks here and it ain't your Eau de Cathouse."

"You need to stop casting aspersions, guy," Gunga said. "I have not been spending the off-season running those Kentucky massage parlors." From April to November every year, Gunga posed as the disreputable owner of a squalid adult drive-in theater south of Bloomington. No clue about his employer. I only knew DEA didn't fit because Petey the Pecker operated with impunity. Where Gunga traveled during the winter months was also a mystery to me. I'd learned long ago not to pry.

"Sucks to be you," I said. "After you've got the dope on Daddy Lungs, hightail it back to Bloomington and start checking out people Elizabeth might know locally. I want to fly below radar so I don't burn my chances of getting Angie back unharmed. But I will put my favorite mole to work on university records for the two students."

"Lady Divine?" Gunga asked. He cringed as I just missed winging some dipshit on a skateboard.

"Only the best. You mind doing the interviews? I think it's safe enough for me to buttonhole Vinnie about his asshole cousin, but I want to steer clear of anyone the Pecker might connect with Elizabeth."

Gunga nodded somberly, all business now. "So who do you have in mind locally?"

"Elizabeth lives on the first floor of a house at 506 Prow Avenue. Name on the mailbox for the upstairs tenant is Luna Lebouche."

"You're shitting me," he laughed.

"No, honestly, chief, that's her name. Find out if she noticed anything hinky going on with Elizabeth in the last week or so."

"Leave it to me, Brother Oz," he said. "Just as long as she doesn't have poisoned areolae."

"Amen to that," I breathed. I swung the Red Baron through the turnaround in front of the old HoJo's from Walnut to College. Town had too many one-way streets. "I hope my Diner's Club doesn't reject the charge for the car, amigo."

Gunga hauled a wallet out of his battered fishing vest. "I'm filing this visit as a sweep for possible foreign terrorists. God's truth for a change. Man upstairs will give me carte blanche," he said. "Besides, your cheap ass would stick me in a subcompact,and Uncle Gunga is all about creature comforts these days."

As I pulled into the Enterprise parking lot, Gunga put his head down and cleaned his glasses with a loose shirttail. "Ozzie, I gotta tell you, something is eatin' me about this scene," he said.

"Welcome to the club," I said. "I haven't had a case go to hell so quickly since I became a civilian."

He put his specs back on. "Stop avoiding the elephant in the room, guy. In a matter of a few short hours, Dza-lu passes up perfect opportunities to put each of us underground. You wanna tell me why he came so close without turning our lights off?"

I grabbed my keys from the ignition and sucked on my upper lip. "Best I can figure it, amigo? The old bastard has something extra special planned for our demise."

Gunga exited the car with a loud grunt and stopped me from opening the rental car office door. "Then we don't give him another swing at us, right, guy?" he said. "You steer clear of the extracurriculars until this is over? And for fuck's sake, get rid of the hospital bracelet, Oz. You look like an escapee from the mental ward."

Christ, I thought. Had everyone on this planet forgotten how to have fun?

All sorts of dark images gnawed at my guts as I headed east out Third Street, not the least of which was Gunga's mention of Dza-lu and the box of Ho-Hos I'd bought at the downtown Kroger. The Ho-Hos formed a ghastly wax ball right over my pyloric valve. I could see Dza-lu's malevolent features etched on the hood of my car. I'd been waiting almost half my life for this confrontation, and now that facing the bastard again was a tangible reality, I was coming down with the yips.

Dza-lu and his enigmatic Dutch partner, Lodewyck van Keel, had commandeered an army of Chiang Kaichek's ex-Kuomintang soldiers somewhere at the heart of the Golden Triangle in the early '60s. Frank Knight, Gunga, and I had originally been sent from Laos to liaise with a Thai border police team in '67. The scope of our assignment expanded when some dimwit at Langley divined that Dza-lu supported the Pathet Lao and possibly the VC with heroin money. Everyone in-country knew that was crap intelligence, but headquarters would not be contradicted. We busted our humps breaking Dza-lu's grip over the drug routes leading down from Burma's Kentung State. Just before the Tet shit show, we got our break. Van Keel used backchannels to contact Frank and said he wanted out. Dza-lu had become too dangerous and unstable, even for his partner. The Dutchman gave us exact coordinates and times for a direct attack in exchange for what was essentially an extraction of himself and two civilians under his care.

Van Keel and a woman carrying a young child met us at the rendezvous point in a jungle clearing two clicks north of Thailand's Chiang Rai Province. Dza-lu got wind of the Dutchman's defection and was waiting for us as well. We started taking heavy fire from every direction minutes after arriving, nearly wiping out a company of U.S.-trained Hmong guerillas we'd brought with us. We got separated from van Keel in all the chaos. Gunga's report listed him as missing and presumed dead along with the woman and child. Dza-lu then used a barrage of pyrotechnics to slaughter Frank Knight and nearly cripple me, earning him my undying hatred.

41

I never saw Dza-lu wielding a weapon just before the flames engulfed me. He simply pointed a finger at us, and the fire erupted.

I don't know how Gunga and the last few Hmong fighters dragged my shredded corpse back to our outpost at Pa Daet or why I didn't bleed out. My new CO wasn't buying any of my frankly unconventional theories about how Dza-lu massacred us. I was rotated stateside for recovery and then was reassigned to some profound apeshittery now known as MKULTRA. After sixteen months of that circus, I opted for Plan B. I started taking classes at the cheapest law school I could find with an evening division. As soon as I finished, I jumped ship to the Bureau, making myself enemies all over D.C. for showing such disloyalty.

Peter Pecorino was one of Dza-lu's alleged midwest heroin distributors, which never made any sense to me. Why not Chicago, Detroit, or St. Louis? Hell—why not Indianapolis? The Pecker was definitely moving China white, but Gunga and I believed his real job was yours truly. Neon told us Petey had been working odd jobs for his cousin, Vinnie Pecorino, until I retired to Bloomington. Dza-lu put feelers out to the usual suspects looking for someone to keep tabs on me. Vinnie dabbled in drug trafficking, but he wanted nothing to do with what Dza-lu was peddling. He wisely surmised it was high time to go legit and concentrate on his wife's fly-by-night cosmetics business. Petey was all too willing to get in bed with the Devil.

While both the DEA and the Company still placed Dza-lu in the hill country of Burma, Gunga and I were sure that Petey was hiding the bastard somewhere very close to home. Dza-lu had actually visited Bloomington way back in 1975, in the guise of persecuted Tibetan Buddhist monk, Dzogchen Tulku Rinpoche, which was when I first met Buckley. Dza-lu blew town before I could apprehend him. I always had a feeling he'd return to B-town, so I did as well when I'd finally screwed my last pooch with the Bureau.

Returned with a target on my back.

You see, Dza-lu held Gunga and me responsible for his daughter's death in the conflagration that cost Frank Knight his life. We neither met nor laid a hand on the daughter, but Dza-lu left no mistake about why he'd put a million-dollar bounty on each of us. He was also convinced we had beguiled the Dutchman into betraying him.

The motel I used as a safe house was on my way east out Third Street. In retrospect, it was far too public, with both an all-glass check-in area and outside room entrances visible from the road. I could see how a decent shadow might've made Elizabeth and me Tuesday night. I parked the Red Baron and hurried inside to the front desk.

The middle-aged woman working reception was indifferent and monosyllabic. Her name tag identified her as Wanda. She turned downright grumpy when I told her I'd forgotten to check out when I left that morning and had lost the key.

Wanda entered the room number on her computer and said, "You're in luck, Mr. Smith," emphasizing the last name and clearly indicating she knew I'd checked in for some *in flagrante* nookie. "A woman we'll call Mrs. Smith, as a favor, hmmm? She dropped off the key at 10:20 and said she didn't like the room." Wanda made a clucking noise. "You bail without paying the lady, Mr. Smith? Or just too quick on the trigger?"

Should I whip out the amazing mechanical bull ride? No, maintain a low profile at all costs, I'd reminded Neon. Surprised that Pecorino hadn't stolen the rest of Elizabeth's benjamins from my coat pocket, I dangled one in front of Wanda. "I need to know who was on the desk when Mrs. Smith left last night. I won't tell where I got the info." Wanda quickly scribbled a name and number on a piece of paper with the motel's logo and then snatched the bill out of my hand. I like to think I was the first man who made Wanda smile in a very long time.

I hopped back in the Valiant and lead-footed it out Third towards Nashville. In a matter of minutes, the ostentatious half-Tudor exterior of The Hunt Club loomed up on my left just before the turnoff to Lake Monroe, interrupting more grim reveries. I abruptly changed lanes and veered into the parking lot. Sent some frat boy practicing for the Little 5 cartwheeling into a PCB-laced drainage ditch. What kind of idiot rode a bike in this weather?

Since it was just after noon and The Hunt Club didn't open its doors for business until four, I walked around to the rear of the building. One of the beer distributors was delivering kegs. I slipped through the open back entrance and down the kitchen hallway unnoticed by the staff. The Hunt Club was a cut above the usual divey buckets of blood I frequented to drink myself into oblivion and beyond. The interior was dark cherry paneling adorned with big game trophy heads and tarnished flintlocks. At one end of the main room was a long bar wrapped in zebra pelts, and at the other end was a raised stage sporting a baby grand. The resident weeknight attraction was why I was here, and I only needed a minute or two before I located Lady Divine's silky alto in a cluster of back offices.

I'd first met Miss Divine in '88 while investigating the kidnapping of a local radio celebrity, D.J. Panic. Lady was singing at Rico's Monkey Barrel at the time. When I mentioned to Rico that Panic had been involved in some sort of computer gambling ring, the resourceful saloon-keeper revealed that besides having a great set of pipes, Lady was also a hacker of the first water and might be able to help me. Lady eventually moved on to The Hunt Club after Saffire's piano player died in a freak accident with a carpet shampooer. We stayed in touch. She soon taught me how to unofficially access the records of several major credit card companies. As long as I kept bringing her back-issues of Angie's Pudding Pop Weekly and boxes of frozen burritos, we were in business.

I found Lady admiring herself in a full-length mirror in her dressing-room. She was wearing a spandex décolletage which had been dipped in bright purple sequins.

"Subdued, yet forceful," I observed. "A dress that makes a statement—come over here, bud, and jump my bones."

Lady spun around. She uttered a slew of blistering obscenities, then stared pointedly at my empty hands. "Where's the mags and my burritos?"

"Didn't have time," I said, perching on the vanity by the door. "This one's gonna be a favor, Lady. For now, at least."

"Favor, Ozzie? I don't do nobody favors," she reminded me.

I regretfully parted with another one of Elizabeth's hundreds. Promising Angie her back salary may have been the first of many bad moves on this disaster. "That's real harsh of you, considering I saved you from the Goat-girl of Guadalupe."

"Yeah, and took a bullet with my name on it, to boot," she responded. She noticed the dark circles around my bloodshot eyes and maybe even the plastic bracelet I'd yet to remove. "Hey, something bad's eating you, isn't it, Ozzie?"

I pulled a stale El Presidente out of my vest pocket and chewed off the end. "You remember Petey the Pecker?" I asked. The Hunt Club normally catered to moneyed gun nuts that enjoyed hoisting a few and bragging about decimating the local fauna. On Lady Divine's advice, the owners had called me to help escort Pecorino off the premises when he refused to abide by club rules by loudly and publicly advertising for untraceable military hardware. Some trash even their bouncers wouldn't remove. "Well, he's holding my secretary hostage, and I gotta handle this sub rosa."

"My sweet Jesus," Lady Divine said. "Anything I can do to get Angie back, you name it." Please note she did not return the Franklin.

I motioned towards the laptop sitting beside me on the vanity. "I want a run-down on two IU students. The works. Academic records, admissions stuff, everything you can tease out of the system. You up for it?"

"Did the Goat-girl give me crabs?" she chuckled. She shimmied across the floor and waved me away from her make-up table. "Who're the kids?"

"Elizabeth Lungs and Kyle Fiffie." I flashed on Elizabeth's mailbox again. "And maybe look up a Luna Lebouche while you're at it?"

Lady Divine crashed the Recorder's files with practiced ease, her lithe fingers flying across the Toshiba's keyboard. I wanted to hit the bar and pour myself a flagon of The Hunt Club's private label Armagnac, but I could still hear Neon's admonition.

I'd been pacing around the room for about five minutes, generally fouling the atmosphere with my cigar and a couple of robust Ho-Ho eructations, when Lady sang, "Gotcha!"

"What is it?" I asked, leaning over her bare and sumptuous shoulder.

She tapped the monitor with a ruby nail. "You looking down my cleavage, perv?"

"I'd be a fool not to."

"Look at this line instead," she said impatiently. "Lungs and Fiffie both have the same advisor, and they work in the guy's lab."

"J Conradt? Who the hell is he?"

Lady blinked at me. Where did she learn to blink with attitude? "Janos Conradt. These two are in molecular biology, Ozzie. That's Conradt's bag. He's a minor-league deity of DNA splicing. Dreams of building bigger and better transgenic beasties."

"How do you know so much about him?"

"Because Doc Conradt's on our board. Serious hunter. Regular trips to Africa and South America." She frowned. "Now that I think about it, he hangs out here a lot with Timmy Bee and Duane Dorff."

"Former heavy hitters for Petey Pecorino's uncle, if I remember correctly."

"Nothing gets by you, eh, Ozzie?" she said. "Yeah, kind of odd company for a prof."

I rocked back and forth on the heels of my Beatle boots. "I had Kyle down for working with that wacko, Wardigus, over in the School of Music," I said. "Caught him with some stolen antique Prince Alberts in a can. Claimed he was selling 'em for her."

"Looks like Fiffie's burning the candle at both ends, Oz. Master's candidate in musicology with Wardigus but a postdoc in Conradt's lab." She did something with the mouse to highlight Fiffie's name on Elizabeth's file. "Kyle's her lab supervisor. She became a graduate assistant for Conradt last September when she arrived at IU. Originally admitted for comparative languages, switched to biology."

"How often does that happen, Lady?"

She shook her head. "Don't know, but I can ask someone in Graduate Studies."

I squinted at the Toshiba. "Got other addresses on her besides 506 Prow?"

"Nope. That's where the university lists her. Any reason to think otherwise?"

"Probably grasping at straws," I said. "Place was kind of dumpy and didn't match her style. Maybe I'll hit the courthouse and search the address through all the property filings."

Lady had another go at her laptop. "County is light-years away from automating their records, but I do have one place to check if you can hold your horses." She brought up a screen of property listings and scrolled through a lengthy display. "Winner winner chicken dinner," she giggled.

"What have you got?"

"This is IU Real Estate's home, Ozzie. These are all their rentals. They owned 506 but sold it last October."

"Okay, should I be reading anything into this?" I asked.

"You tell me, old man. You're the detective. All I've got is the sale. Nothing about the buyer."

Recorder's was right across the street from my office in the courthouse. Next stop, I thought. "So anything on Lebouche?"

Lady futzed around with the keyboard. "Looks like she just got assigned an IU email address. No status, though. Means she's either a new employee or just enrolled for the spring semester. Takes a while to get everybody in the system."

I switched back to the common denominator. "So why would a molecular biologist like Conradt and his students be screwing around with a hot dinosaur egg?" I wondered aloud.

Lady shook her head, her eyes glued to the screen. Then, she slowly looked up at me, an expression of pure glee creasing her lovely heart-shaped face. "Cloning," she smiled.

"Say what?"

"These crazy kids are looking for a way to bring a dinosaur back to life!"

Five: Do The Humpty-Dumpty

I left The Hunt Club after Lady Divine said she'd need at least a day to worm her way into the IU Bursar's records for anything else suspicious on our pair of Mr. Science alums. She made me swear an oath that I'd bring Angie by once I'd secured her return. That was jake with me. I had no idea of where Angie hid her Pudding Pop porn from me. God knows I'd rifled through her desk for those mags every time she went out to lunch. I doubted if Lady was into bronzed pig nuts, which, at this point, was about all I had to offer her for her services.

As I revved up the Valiant, I experienced that noisome ache I got when a case went sideways. Felt like a long, red-hot poker impaling me from my median sulcus down to the battery powering my handy-dandy penile implant. A wave of nausea crested through my Ho-ho'ed guts as I instantly remembered the ball of fire Dza-lu had propelled through my bulbourethral artery, effectively curtailing my sex life until an unlicensed Swiss surgeon rebuilt my goods.

This dinosaur egg business really threw a leprous hairy armadillo into the works. DNA fingerprinting was the latest forensic technology, but from what I'd read in the DOJ literature Gunga sent my way, you needed pretty fresh bodily fluids. There couldn't be any way Conradt was harvesting DNA from rocks, right? And where the hell did the late Kyle Fiffie fit in this puzzle? I was beginning to suspect that Elizabeth Lungs had a lot more on her mind besides Petey the Pecker and where she was going to find a box of royal blue sanitary napkins.

And always in the back of my mind there was the sound of Angie's terrified voice. Was any more digging going to cost her an arm and a leg? Or a disarticulated spleen, I fretted, recalling just one of Dza-lu's more unsavory methods of dispatching his victims.

Pulling back into my parking space at the office, I nearly squashed a teenaged couple from the sandwich shop downstairs who were devoting their lunch break to a bit of al fresco doggy-style in the alley. My next task was to get big bad Deppity Bob off my back. I toyed with the idea of spot-welding his nose to the 4:15 Greyhound to Evansville, but that might only antagonize the humorless bastard. The most expeditious method of dealing with local law enforcement was to find someone up the food chain to claim jurisdiction and issue a cease and desist.

Time to call in yet another favor. My best shot was an old FBI buddy in the Chicago office since the local Bureau guys had strict instructions to steer clear of my traitorous ass. At the mere mention of The Devil, Special Agent Alexander Skenitis promised he'd read the riot act to Slorby. Alex had been a rookie on field assignment to the Indianapolis office when I first came down to Bloomington and broke up Dza-lu's Tantric fan club.

"So how long does that buy me?" I asked aloud, staring balefully at Angie's empty desk and the answering machine. I kept reminding myself of Gunga's parting remarks about Dza-lu. I had no illusions whatsoever about how the old demon was going to play this routine. Dza-lu had inflicted more monstrously slow and agonizing deaths than I knew ways to make any woman beg me to leave her alone.

Without even thinking, I opened the closet in the reception area where Angie kept office supplies and snagged a bottle of Australian gin I kept for special emergencies. A bloom of turpentine and rancid kangaroo piss filled the room, nearly dislodging those Ho-hos.

Maybe Neon and Gunga had the right idea. Getting bent probably wasn't the best strategy against the necromancer, but it was the only remedy I knew for the endless remorse I'd suffer if I could never be reminded of bing cherries when I walked into the office on a cold and otherwise cheerless morning. I put the bottle back in the closet and sagged down at my desk.

No new calls on the answering machine meant Neon had yet to find anything remarkable on Fiffie's murder. Nor had Angie's kidnappers seen fit to let me off the hook, although I fully expected they'd keep me dangling at least until Dza-lu figured out how to exterminate Gunga and me at the same time. I was saving my surprise visit to Vinnie Pecorino's establishment until a few minutes before five that evening, leaving me plenty of time to mosey across the street to the Monroe County courthouse and go annoy some hapless civil servants. I retrieved a pen and legal pad from the supply closet and walked back out into the frigid slop.

If I'd learned anything during nearly sixteen hellish years as a federal investigator, it was to never dismiss a coincidence. Sure, Frank Knight had also threatened to tattoo "Correlation does not constitute causation" on my forehead, but Elizabeth Lungs' rental changing hands less than two months after she enrolled was too much of a red flag for my money.

Poring through deed records, real estate transfers, and property assessments was about the lowest form of gumshoe drudgery next to trolling accident scenes for the town's biggest ambulance chaser. At least going undercover as the topless show-shine girl earned me tax-free tips. A lot more dough than the disguise warranted, but there's no accounting for tastelessness. I usually sent Angie over for a mind-numbing day tackling the massive volumes of land transactions. Not an option today. Having an address and a pretty narrow window on the sale of the house on Prow made the task a little more straightforward, but even a few minutes navigating the faint, computer-generated indexes rekindled my lingering headache. I kind of doubted any of the cardiganed old ladies in the recorder's office had a Demerol between them, so I soldiered on. Fortunately for everyone in the room, I hit pay dirt before I started throwing a tantrum.

The recording of the mortgage showed that 506 North Prow Avenue had been sold by the Indiana University Foundation to a couple named Poul and Celine Monny on October 19th of last year. "Poul" struck me as odd. Wasn't there a science fiction writer with that first name? The couple gave their address as a post office box in Bloomington and financed the purchase through a local bank not half a block away from the courthouse and my office. I wrote down the pertinents in my clearest block lettering, then paid a ridiculous dollar per page to copy everything on an old wheezing Minolta.

Finding little more than names and a P.O. box number left me feeling about as empty as I did after jerking off to my high school yearbook's photo of Cheryl Funt, the girls' gym teacher. Which I had totally stopped doing. This year. So far. As I hefted the October 1990 volume back up on its shelf, I wondered if I knew anyone at the bank I could convince to look the other way while I lifted Social Security numbers and birthdates off the Monnys' mortgage application. There was no way Neon would ask the bank for permission to check their records without a warrant. My best bet for a gander at the bank's file would be to promise Tripp Crossman down the hall that I'd do my next gig in exchange for the Monnys' vitals. Another item on my to-do list.

Since I still had over an hour to kill before I headed over to Vinnie's office, I chased down some of the other names I'd collected so far. Got bupkis on Fiffie. Made sense—he was a student and most likely renting. Ditto on Conradt, which seemed worth noting if Lady Divine had correctly pegged him as a hotshot. Elizabeth Lungs may have also been leasing her crib, but she occupied center square and I couldn't leave without searching her.

I can't remember the last time I pitched a tent over something as dry and prosaic as a property filing. When I discovered a second mortgage recorded for one Leon Lungs from the same bank handling 506 North Prow, I started moaning loud enough to make one of the biddies call security. That loan was finalized on October 12th, 1990. "Just found my long lost son!" I laughed, which probably made everyone feel a lot worse about the projection in my pants.

The second mortgage was on a house on Holly Lane, one of many streets in Bloomington I'd never heard of. A quick study of a huge Monroe County wall map on the other side of the office revealed Holly Lane was in a wooded area just north of Lake Monroe, probably overlooking the reservoir. Private getaway or possibly a summer vacation home for the Carmel colostomy bag king? Tracing Leon's acquisition of the Holly Lane property took almost as long as the rest of my courthouse fishing expedition. I finally located the January 8, 1975 record. Lungs appeared to already be living at the Holly Lane address when the sale went through. There was no mention of Carmel. I'd never heard of the mortgagee bank, an organization called Hallum Trust, so I wrote that on the legal pad as well. I blew another few bucks photocopying both of the Leon Lungs transactions and packed up.

According to my watch, I still had long enough to go bug Crossman for the mortgage application. Then I got a wild hair about Mr. and Mrs. Monny and how I could avoid horse-trading with Tripp. I dashed out of the courthouse and made a beeline north on College to the Monroe County Justice Center. It felt a little weird not checking a firearm with the officer manning the metal detector at the

Center's entrance. Bopping around unarmed in public was a phenomenally boneheaded move if Dza-lu was closing in. I wondered if Slorby's bulls had swiped the Smith and Wesson Chief's Special taped under the front seat of the Valiant when they towed it last night.

The guy at the County Clerk's Office desk knew me from an insurance fraud case I'd worked a few months ago. I'd cemented our acquaintance with an under-the-counter single malt gratuity for not making me jump through the usual hoops. Today I made him the same offer for any October 1990 marriage license papers for Poul and Celine Monny that he might accidentally drop in my hands. It was a half-baked gamble and would cost me money I did not have to throw around, but I thought why not shoot for the trifecta. I stood to one side to let the person behind me come up to the window. Before I had a chance to reexamine the copies I'd made at the Recorder's, my new best friend pushed a single sheet of paper my way. An attached note listed the best days and times to deliver a plain-wrapper package.

The marriage of Poul Monny and Celine Bell, both of Bloomington, had been solemnized October 12, 1990, right here in the Clerk's Office. Way beyond a coincidence, I wanted to scream. Next thing I noticed was a sizeable age gap between the two. Poul had been born in Indianapolis in 1935 and Celine in Noblesville in 1972. Poul, you cradle-robbing dog! Wish I'd been standing in line when he waltzed in with his barely legal bride-to-be. I really wanted to make a copy of the license application. There were three other people waiting for the photocopier and it was now 4:25. I scribbled as much from the original as I thought would help me, then returned the document to my lifelong buddy, giving him a thumbs up.

Whenever someone on television gets clobbered unconscious, the victim invariably shakes off the injury in a few seconds and jumps back into action. Like everything else you see on the tube, it just ain't so. Pounding down the block and a half to my parking space was killing my head. Once I was in the car, I double-checked my eyes in the rearview mirror to make sure my pupils were the same size. They looked normal to me. The gnawing void in my stomach reassured me that I wasn't going to die from a subdural hematoma. Better yet, I reached under my seat and found the snub-nosed .38. Could I improve on this afternoon? Getting Angie back in one piece and falling over Dza-lu's corpse in the alley would be nice. Until then, I'd settle for bracing Vinnie Pecorino about his dickhead cousin.

After my initial encounter with the Pecorinos in 1987, Neon explained that Vinnie and Petey's grandfather had been a foot soldier in the Castellamarese War. He allegedly clipped the wrong guy and got sent to the boonies to fade the heat. Old Man Pecorino's original plan once he hit town had been to prey on fellow citizens of Italian descent. A lot of these guys were hard-working and hard-headed stonecutters who'd moved to Indiana to quarry limestone, so that didn't pan out. Lacking any other legitimate marketable skills, Pecorino finally found his niche hauling bootleg liquor up from the Ohio River counties of Indiana and Kentucky. Once Prohibition ended, he branched out into book-making, prostitution, narcotics, and playing the protection racket with vulnerable small business owners. His sons added truck hijacking and auto theft to the family portfolio. Neon said there were also rumors of contract killings, that Petey's dad got his head blown off during a botched job. All the witnesses skedaddled, and none of the Pecorinos ever got sent away for murder. I planned on reversing that trend.

It was pretty much gospel that Valerie Pecorino's beauty supply company, Simply Too Gorgeous, started out as a tax dodge and a place for Vinnie to wash and rinse contaminated assets. Vinnie wisely chose survival over traditional Pecorino family values when Dza-lu's creatures issued him an ultimatum on the local hard drug trade and now devoted himself full time to Valerie's hobby shop.

Simply Too Gorgeous operated out of a concrete block strip mall behind Western Skate Land on West Seventeenth Street. As far as anyone could tell, all Simply Too Gorgeous actually did was repackage cut-rate Chinese cosmetics no one in her right mind would buy, then foisted the toxic spew off on larger unsuspecting suppliers. I had no idea how they avoided the wrath of the FDA and any hungry products liability mouthpiece. But who am I to judge? Vinnie was doing far less harm hawking this gunk than peddling heroin, crack, and meth like his cousin, Petey.

Place must not get a lot of foot traffic, I thought as I opened the door. I found Vinnie trading spit with a gorgeous blonde I recognized as Valerie's best friend, Felicity Goss. She was sitting at one of three desks in the front of an office suite and was dressed in a blue and white cheerleader's uniform. I assumed the letters STG were emblazoned across the chest. Couldn't be certain, though, because Vinnie was cupping her right breast. I also assumed the Pecorinos had arrived at some sort of understanding because Valerie occupied one of the other desks. She also wore a cheerleading outfit.

"Go team," I leered, intentionally addressing Valerie while her husband walked off his tumescence. "What's hot these days in the world of feminine pulchritude?"

Valerie was an axed-face brunette with big eyes and even bigger hair. Neon told me she came from Pentecostal stock and had initially made Vinnie's rehabilitation her life's work. Must've lost her way somewhere between the artificial nails and a ménage a trois with Felicity. "We're getting into flavored douches," she said, holding up the plastic pouches of brightly colored fluid she was permasealing into larger Simply Too Gorgeous envelopes. "This is my favorite— White Grenache."

"Don't mind me, Vinnie," I said over my shoulder, as he hastily shuffled over to the third desk. "What's this one"? I asked, holding up a bag of hazy golden goo.

"We're thinking of calling it Bush Light. For the bowlers in the family," Felicity said.

"But Vinnie thinks we'll get in trouble for that," Valerie added.

To my credit, I didn't whoop "no fucking shit," instead making with "He may have a point."

Vinnie Pecorino was an even shorter, fatter, and uglier version of Petey the Pecker. He looked like a hairy carp seen through a beer mug, and that's being cruel to the carp. I didn't understand how the opposite sex could find him appealing. I didn't want to, either.

"Don't try to patronize me, shitballs," Vinnie rasped.

"Shitballs? After all our good times?" I tried to sound hurt without laughing. "After I saved you from the Goat-girl of Guadalupe?"

Apparently the hunk of lead I'd intercepted on his behalf didn't count. "Your little stooge, Knight, has already grilled me about my retarded cousin, so get the fuck outta here, Yesterday!" he squawked. "It's five o'clock and we're shuttin' down."

I didn't want to waste another benjamin on Vinnie, so I flashed him the .38 instead. Very subtle, though, so as not to give Valerie and Felicity the vapors. "The lieutenant and I haven't found time to compare notes," I said. "You got somewhere private we can reconnoiter?" I tipped my Vicks-flecked Borsalino to the women. "No offense, ladies."

"None taken," Felicity replied. I liked the twinkle in her eye, but Vinnie might not appreciate me saying so.

"This way, cunt," he snarled, then mockingly added, "No offense, bitches." Vinnie clenched his jowls and indicated that I should follow him through the single door to the rear of the complex.

The back room was a poorly-lit corridor that had been studded out, forgotten, and then filled with flimsy metal shelves stacked with product. A woman in her late teens with the sad misfortune of resembling Vinnie was listlessly dumping CBT dross into a cardboard box. "Hey, Muffie," Vinnie said, "grab your coat and go tell your mother it's quittin' time. Gimme two minutes with this douchebag, and I'll meet you in the car."

I wanted to tell Vinnie "douchebag" wasn't a very nice word to use around his daughter, but they probably sold those, too. Muffie executed a fine adolescent eye-roll. She pulled a fake fox car coat off a hanger near the door and slouched out. "Nice kid," I told Vinnie.

"Go fuck yourself, Yesterday," he spat back. "You don't get to look at my daughter!" Vinnie was really winding himself up. His swarthy face flushed almost purple and a tic jolted the outer corner of his left eye. "I'll tell you exactly what I told your pet pig. I haven't seen Petey since my wife went soft and invited him to Christmas dinner. I want nothin' to do with his affairs, you hear me, asshole? I don't want to even know that cokehead, you got it?"

"Or the company he keeps, Vinnie?"

Walking behind Vinnie to the storeroom, I'd spotted the piece stuffed under the back of his garish Hawaiian shirt and leather vest. He made his move but was so out of practice that I had the .38 jammed in his thicket of a beard before he could wrestle his pistol free.

"Vinnie, don't ever think of drawing down on me again," I said. "Getting your skull aired out over a simple question from a friend would be a damn stupid way to die."

"You ain't no friend of mine," Vinnie rumbled between clenched teeth. "And neither is Petey or that fuckin' animal pullin' his strings!"

The door from the front of the office swung open. Felicity gawked at us with widened summer sky-blue eyes. "Sorry, boys," she said. "Just getting Valerie's coat!"

I quickly dropped the .38 in my coat pocket. "No problem, ma'am," I said. "We've about wrapped up our delightful little chat." Felicity definitely gave me a wink this time and made a hasty exit.

"Thanks for the dance, Vinnie," I chuckled. "I'm sure Lieutenant Knight already told you to contact him in the event you do hear from Petey, right?"

"Yeah, I'll do that, turdo," he husked, fighting the adrenaline spike. Roughing up Vinnie in front of one of his women probably soured our wonderful rapport, but at least he didn't reach for his gun again. Just to be on the safe side, I backed out of the storeroom and left him leaning with his hands on his knees to catch his breath.

Valerie silently glared eternal damnation at me when I touched my hat brim goodbye to her. Muffie had plugged into a Walkman and floated out across another universe. Felicity returned to her desk to continue work on the pussy wash.

"I'll lock up when you leave," she told Valerie. "I want to finish these before I head home." In case I didn't get the message, Felicity winked at me as Valerie rose from her chair. Seeing as I wasn't going to collect any fond farewells from the Pecorinos, I went out to my car.

Instead of heading back east on Seventeenth to the office, I turned north onto Willis Drive from the strip mall parking lot and did a few laps around the mobile home park at the end of the street. I was wishing I'd booked a rental myself. A thirty-year-old crimson bomber with a rusty front exhaust pipe wasn't the most surreptitious ride. I guessed Vinnie planned on heading out as quickly as possible for some ethanol relief, but I still gave myself a good fifteen minutes before I parked the Valiant in front of Simply Too Gorgeous again. Felicity was waiting at the door for me and unlocked it as I walked up.

"Is it safe?" I said in my best German accent. I don't think Felicity was an Olivier fan. She let me in any way, grabbed my arm, and hustled me back to the storeroom.

"Oh. My. God!" she exclaimed after she'd lit a cigarette from a pack in her coat. "What did Vinnie do to provoke that shit?"

"You know him well, and not just in the Biblical sense," I grinned. "This thing with his cousin has got him spooked. I made the mistake of getting cute about it. My bad." I gestured for a hit off her Marlborough. "So is he telling the truth about not seeing Petey?"

"Valerie and Vinnie are my best friends," she said, but she didn't appear to be insulted. Felicity's cupid bow mouth curled into a momentary pout. She was at least a head taller than me even without her pair of five-inch black stiletto heels. She wore her blonde hair in large yet tasteful waves. "I feel for Petey. He's messed up bad. On the other hand, he's nice to me. He shares treats. On the house, y'know?"

I nodded and finished the cigarette for her. "I got no problem with recreational use, but I'm betting you know Cousin Petey works for a maniac who makes Vinnie and me look like teddy bears."

"Awww, do you have a warm furry side too, Mr. Yesterday?" she said with a smile that almost made me forget why I'd returned.

"They don't come any furrier," I murmured. I needed to work on my come-on lines. That was weird. And given Vinnie's hirsuteness, a blatant lie. "So, uh, Petey," I said. "When was the last time you saw him?"

Felicity was still making with the high-voltage smile although she gave me a straight answer. "Vinnie's got big problems with Petey, but Valerie insists on having everyone in the family over for dinner every Sunday night. He didn't show this Sunday, and he knows enough to call Valerie if he can't make it or is in no shape to be around Vinnie." She took my Borsalino off my head and put it on one of the shelves behind her. "Not a word from him all weekend. Vinnie tries not to make a big deal about it. I know he's worried sick." She craned her neck and gave me a heart-stopping open-mouth kiss.

I could not remember the last time a woman got the hots for me because I pulled a gun on her man. Or maybe Felicity just had a thing for butt-ugly short guys.

Going for nonchalant, I laughed and said, "So what's with the outfits?"

Felicity laughed as well. "Valerie told Vinnie I was a cheerleader in high school. Turns out cheerleaders were one of his many unfulfilled fantasies, so he bought the uniforms for us both and slapped on the logo."

What the hell, I thought. "A lot of guys have the same fantasy, babe. Can you still do the splits?"

"I think you'll like this even better." She hiked up the short skirt a little and said, "Plant your feet steady, Mr. Yesterday." In one fluid motion, she raised her right leg and rested it on my left shoulder.

"Limber," I managed to say without salivating on my chest. How the fuck did she pull that off in those fetish heels?

"Just getting warmed up," Felicity purred. She looked me in the eyes very seriously then balanced her right foot on my Nietzsche tattoo. "Ta-daa!" she sang. I was staring directly into the crotch of her blue uniform shorts. Her legs were deeply tanned and smelled faintly of strawberries. "Now for my next trick," she said. She squeezed her eyes shut and inched forward. She finished with the back of her knee on top of my head.

Having come this far, I said, "We were always told only the slutty cheerleaders didn't wear panties under their bloomers."

"You were told absolutely right," she sighed. She pulled the shorts to one side, revealing her recently shaved and glistening vulva. I required no additional encouragement. Supporting her leg with my left hand, I squatted down and buried my face in her fragrant pussy. I had no problem finding her erect clit and circled it with my tongue, licking slowly and intently. Felicity moaned and wrapped her fingers around my ears.

After her first orgasm, she panted, "You seem to know your way around these parts!"

"Everybody's gotta be good at something," I said.

Felicity pawed at my head again and told me, "That's our strawberry daiquiri flavored one!"

"I'm sure it is," I mumbled as I went in for a second helping.

Six: As A Weasel Sucks Eggs

Waking up in my own bed sober and without a fatal hangover was a novel experience. I wasn't exactly overjoyed about doing it alone, but bringing Felicity back to an apartment decked out with rotting meat and fermented vomit didn't feel right, even for a one night stand. Sure, a bed or even a carpeted floor would've prevented some of the glorious bruises we gave each other in Simply Too Gorgeous's shipping department the night before. Both of us, however, were veteran horn-dogs, so we improvised. It was after 9 p.m. when we agreed to stop before we killed each other.

"Whoever built this machine deserves a medal," she said, appreciatively dandling my bionic dingus. "Felt like you were taking a Sawzall to my cervix."

"Is that a good thing?"

She gave me a weary smile and asked if I had a business card on me. Then she cracked me up by insisting we smoke the rest of her cowboy reds to cover up the sex funk.

"It's not like they won't know what you've been doing," I'd said. "You're black and blue, covered in bite marks, and full of cum."

Felicity yawned as she wriggled into the top of her cheerleading uniform. "We're not what you'd call exclusive, but Vinnie'll take it personally if I'm screwing anyone else on company property."

I told her I could understand that. Then I wondered if Angie had ever entertained guests at the office. I didn't think I cared. My value system is pretty elastic and I honestly did not give a shit how people used their genitals so long as they were consenting adults. We're just badly trained animals, right? Had this attitude in any way contributed to the explosive denouement of each of my four marriages? A subject, perhaps, for another time.

My biggest problem with confronting unfiltered reality is that it's uglier than the inside of a barracks latrine and often smells a hundred times worse. Or wurst, I thought, remembering the nightmare awaiting my cleaning service in the bathroom. I really did not want to go in there, but I'd collapsed in bed without showering Wednesday night. The heavenly perfume of Felicity's pudendal strawberry daiquiri gravy had curdled into something so mephitic that not even the flies buzzing around my apartment would light upon.

Oh, wait. It was February. No flies. Maybe this crap weather was good for something after all.

A putty knife would've been the best tool for tackling the green minty gruel crystalizing on the floor around the toilet, but I hadn't replaced the one I used to subdue the Goat-girl of Guadalupe. Rooting around in the vanity cabinet, I found a gallon of bleach I kept for emergency policing (or, more accurately, de-policing) crime scenes and sloshed a quart over the hazard area. I wasn't too concerned about leakage to the apartment below because I knew from a little hole drilled through my bedroom floor that the guy downstairs shot pornos. He could care less what got splattered where.

That reminded me—I'd have to tell Gunga to steal me the newest generation miniature video rig. Strictly for professional purposes.

I did my best to ignore the nameless brown sludge on my shower curtain as I sadly scrubbed all the Felicity away. Maybe I was being too squeamish. Most of that charcuterie was packed with enough nitrates to preserve it until doomsday.

Once I'd washed, dried, and dressed, I got the dustpan along with some old plastic take-out bags from the kitchen closet. That bleach-soaked puke loaf wasn't going to launch itself out the window. Sticking my courage to the screwing place, I held my breath and scooped up as much as I could shovel into the bags. By the time I was done, you still wouldn't have wanted to eat off my bathroom floor, but it put to shame the gas station restroom where my firstborn was conceived.

This new Ozzie apparently could not stomach the bulging plastic bags sitting in the apartment one more minute, so I got dressed and limped down the three flights of stairs to the dumpster in the alleyway. Sobriety hadn't erased all my bad habits—on my way back up, I stopped on the second-floor landing to lift a different neighbor's Bloomington Herald-Times. A quick glance at the headlines told me the police had contacted Kyle Fiffie's next of kin. His name and a photo of him in costume from an IU production of La Bohème splashed the front page. Story said to contact Neon with any information.

I'd just turned to the continuation of the story on Page A3 when I heard the front door from Walnut Street open. Two pairs of footsteps clacking through the tiled entry past the mailboxes and towards the stairs. One male voice whispering. A fine time for my .38 to still be shoved in the pocket of my trench coat. I also kept a small arsenal in the bedroom closet. Lot of good the hardware was doing me now. I knew how to inflict significant damage with a rolled-up newspaper; getting up to the apartment ASAP felt like a safer option.

I hit the stairs hard. The instant I bolted, so did one of the goons a flight below. Dza-lu must've sent someone younger than me with longer legs because he'd already turned the landing on the second floor before I'd reached the third. Those Marlboros last night were going to cost me my life. At least I'd enjoyed one last quality lay.

Neon Knight called "Jesus, Ozzie, it's me!" just as I snatched at the doorknob to my apartment. He took the last few stairs at a normal clip while I slumped in front of my door, my chest heaving for air. Neon wasn't even winded, the bastard.

He pointed at the newspaper. "You left your apartment unarmed? Are you in the bag already?"

"I fucking wish," I gasped. "I run on automatic when I'm tanked. Second day I've spent on the wagon, second day I've gone out without a weapon."

Neon laughed. "So, what, you're like one of those cretins who claim they drive better when they're drunk?"

I wiped a few loose strands of hair back over my scalp. "Works for me." I stood up without vomiting or blacking out, which felt like an accomplishment. "Hope you had a damn good reason for almost giving me a coronary."

He tapped me on the chest. "I have someone you need to listen to. Your office was closed up. Thought I'd try you here."

"Sure, just as long as your pal isn't a neat freak. Cleaning service doesn't come until next Monday."

Neon walked back down to the entryway to retrieve the other guy. I lurched into my kitchen and started making a pot of coffee. I was emptying a tin of Folger's on top of Tuesday morning's mildewed ground when I looked up to see a trim, smiling man with a closely-clipped beard and wire-rimmed glasses follow Neon into my living room. He wore a Harris tweed jacket over a v-neck sweater, a striped scarf, ironed jeans, and carried a worn leather briefcase in one hand and a silver-handled cane in the other.

He sat down in the only chair that wasn't stacked with somebody else's newspapers and my wardrobe. He sniffed disapprovingly at the lingering stench. "Has someone been curing hog meat in here, Osborne?" he asked.

"Gee, it's good to see you again, Ethan," I said. "Why don't you make yourself at home?"

"No need to be so sarcastic, Osborne," he scolded, peering at me like a disappointed schoolmaster. "We're all friends here. As you should recall, my wife saved you from the Goat-girl of Guadalupe." Ethan Nangle was married to Judge Katherine Grange, and he reminded me how much I owed her, and therefore him, every time we saw each other.

"And took a slug with your name on it, to boot," I replied. I'd just smashed through the window to Judge Grange's chambers and tried to draw fire from the Goat-girl. Nangle had been too busy screaming to take cover. The judge dove in between us. She got hit in the hip. I hurled the putty knife at the Goat-girl and caught her square in the forehead. Non-fatal blow, but her left and right cerebral hemispheres got summarily divorced.

"Have it your way," Ethan said with a smug expression on his face that made me want to yank out his tongue. "I have something, or rather, a lot of somethings I think you'll find elucidating."

"Just tell Ozzie what you told me," Neon patiently instructed.

"Very well, Lieutenant. You see, I'm here about an egg."

My hands flew to my mouth in an abortive attempt to keep my upper partial from flying out across the living room. Ethan bent down, plucked the errant piece of dental work from beneath his chair, and handed it to me. I thought he was going to hurl when I pulled part of a cockroach out from between my artificial incisors.

"Did he say egg?" I asked Neon. "Does everybody in this damn city know about the egg?"

"I should apologize for putting such a scare into you," Ethan said although he didn't seem sorry enough. "I assure you that Lieutenant Knight is the only person I've told about the egg."

Neon nodded to confirm. "Ethan came down to the station voluntarily when he read this morning's story about the Fiffie murder. Said he was a friend of the deceased."

"How did you know Fiffie?" I said

"Kyle and I both belong to the same secret society."

"Secret society?" I whimpered. Could the shit get any deeper?

"We're Yes fans," Nangle proudly admitted. "I happen to be the vice-president of the Indiana chapter of the Fraternal Order of Jon Anderson Mavens."

"Dear God! Not FOJAM?!"

Neon excused himself to go pour a cup of coffee. I reckoned he didn't want Nangle to see him shaking with laughter.

"The same," Nangle said without an ounce of shame. "But this business of the egg touches upon another organization to which I belong. Have you ever heard of the Collegial Association of Cornish Antiquarians?"

"No, but I've got a sneaking suspicion I'm going to."

"Don't sound so dismal, Mr. Yesterday. What I am about to tell you will add an entirely new dimension to your current investigation."

I leaned back against the return between the living room and kitchen, cursing my parents for not using a more reliable form of birth control. "Ethan, buddy, this case has so many dimensions that it would make Einstein's head spin."

"Be that as it may, I think you will be intrigued." He went all smug and pompous on us again. Too bad my trench coat and the .38 were in a chair across the room. "What, pray tell, do you know about one St. Keyne?"

"Who's he?"

"She," he said. Nangle scrunched up his eyes and began reciting with condescending forbearance. "St. Keyne? Alternately known as Cain, Ceinwyn or Ceyn-Wyryf, which is Welsh for Keyne the Virgin? Lived in the sixth century, daughter of King Brychan of Brecknock? Aunt of St. Cadoc, probably killed by Saxons about, ohhh, 560, along with the rest of her family? That St. Keyne?"

"Ethan, I jettisoned what little I learned about the Church when my mother died and I moved back to Arizona with the old man's people. I never made a very good mackerel snapper." Didn't make a very good member of the Nde either, but that was old news.

"Why am I not surprised?" Ethan grinned. If he gave me that know-it-all face one more time, I was going to send him back to Judge Grange a boy soprano. I think Neon would've helped me at that point, although he may have been choking on the coffee. Shit. I never had a problem using moldy grounds.

"So you don't know the story of St. Keyne and the serpents of Somerset?" I shook my head no, casually strolling over to pick up my trench coat. I sat down and laid it across my lap. Nangle was already too invested in his exposition to notice.

"Well, when St. Keyne left Wales and crossed the Severn, she made a hermitage for herself in the forests of Somerset, close by the town of Keynsham, which was named after her. John of Tynemouth wrote that the place was infested with serpents and that she turned them to stone. Mum was British, and on our last trip back together, I visited Keynsham. There are quarries nearby where miners found fossils called ammonites and identified them as the eggs of the serpents St. Keyne defeated. Now, today, when we read of serpents and saints driving them out, we naturally think of snakes."

"Like St. Patrick and no snakes in Ireland, right?" Neon asked.

"Precisely!" he exclaimed. Little bits of saliva sprayed over his beard. "But the serpents St. Keyne vanquished were not snakes!"

"Uh-huh," I incitefully posited. "And what has all this to do with the price of eggs, Nangle?"

His eyes fairly sparkled behind the thick lenses of his spectacles. "Ahh, it has everything to do with the price of a certain egg, Mr. Yesterday. You see, the serpents referred to in Tynemouth's "Acta Sanctorum" were dragons! Dragons, I tell you, the physical manifestation of Lucifer! And the dragons St. Keyne conquered were a female demon named Kur-ah-desh and her freshly hatched clutch of young! But the last of the eggs had not yet hatched, and St. Keyne carried this bound and calcified egg with her when she moved from Somerset to the Bodmin Moors in Cornwall. The egg and an ancient parchment describing her battle with Kur-ah-desh remained hidden in a shrine among the tors near the hamlet of St. Keyne until 1936, when both the document and the egg disappeared!"

The bottles of bargain bin joy juice in the cabinet beneath the kitchen sink screamed at me. "Well, now that you've educated us both about this mythical dragon's egg and St. Keyne, what's the connection to Fiffie's death?" I asked.

"As I told the lieutenant, Kyle was well aware of my interest in British antiquities. All I can talk about, to be honest." I almost said you're joking, but I didn't want to draw out this torture any longer than necessary. "At our year-end Yes society meeting in December, he gave me this!" Ethan opened up his briefcase and handed me two pieces of white legal-sized paper. "Don't you see, Osborne? That's a photocopy of the missing St. Keyne parchment! I phoned the president of CACA when Kyle showed it to me and—"

"Caca?" I asked.

"The Collegial Association of Cornish Antiquarians," Neon recited. I wondered how many times he'd heard the name this morning.

"Very good, Lieutenant!" Ethan might have been giving a biscuit to a dog that performed tricks. "Our president agreed that this is The Song of St. Keyne! Don't you understand, Mr. Yesterday? Kyle had access to the original! And once you've recovered that venerable parchment, I must get it back for the people of Cornwall!"

I squinted at the copy of what appeared to be a stained and torn manuscript. The only letters I could recognize were "u-m" at the end of the word, so I was assuming Latin.

Neon brought me a mug of oily brown liquid. "Nice job letting a civilian walk around with a piece of evidence," I scowled at him.

"Give me some credit," Neon said. "That's a Xerox of the copy Ethan brought in with him this morning. Matches this copy of what we found when we searched the trunk of Fiffie's car." He pulled an unsealed legal envelope out of his departmental issue overcoat. I put my coffee cup on the floor to study the second document. Both copies looked identical except for two weird little squiggles on the top of one of the pages Neon had brought along.

"What the hell is this?" I asked, pointing at the marks. Leave no stone unturned, they taught us at Langley.

Ethan got up from his chair and gazed over my shoulder for a good half minute. "We can rule out anything from the original parchment," he murmured, and then, "Why, It's Russian, I believe! The initials W.C.!"

I did my best to suppress a loud guffaw. "That so? Mean anything to you?"

He looked back and forth between Neon and me, then snapped his fingers. "Walker Chumbley! The ex-priest!" he declared. "An ex-priest and an expert on the Dark Ages! I'll wager you Fiffie took the parchment to Chumbley to get it translated from the Latin!"

"Sounds plausible," I said, very serious. "Now I suppose the lieutenant here told you that Fiffie dropped the egg before he was killed? The thing shattered. Here there be no dragons."

Neon cleared his throat. "You need to check your answering machine, Oz," he said. "Bob's people were poking around this thing before somebody called the dogs off." I bet Neon got an earful from Slorby when Alex elbowed him out. "The egg Fiffie broke was stolen from a display case in Jordan Hall. It wasn't even a dinosaur egg. Partially fossilized dodo egg. And pretty damn valuable on its own."

"A pittance compared to the historical and cultural value of St. Keyne's egg!" Ethan asserted. He started in on another blather about the priceless relic. I caught movement from Neon's side of the room. He was drawing his index finger across his throat.

I did a double-take at my watch and pretended to be flustered. "Ethan, I'm sorry," I lied, "but I've got an appointment and I think the lieutenant needs to bring me up to date on the investigation. If you happen to remember anything else important, please make sure and see Detective Knight, okay?"

Nangle seemed crestfallen now that his moment in the spotlight was over. Didn't give up without a fight, though, and he told each of us his phone number, email address, and blood type a dozen times. He alt last relented and allowed me to show him the way out.

I listened to his footsteps descending the stairs, then bolted the door. I turned to Neon and could tell he was pissed about my radio silence yesterday. "So let me get this straight," I said. "Fiffie brought a poached egg to the meet?"

"Save that bullshit for Phemister." Humorless prig. I'd been waiting years to use a line like that. "Where the hell have you been since I put you back in your rust bucket?"

I didn't see any sense in delaying the inevitable, so I unloaded about Angie's kidnapping and Gunga's getting waylaid. The next few minutes marked a low ebb in our quasi-father-son relationship. Neon had some choice words on the subject of not involving the cops and even harsher language on my failure to immediately alert him that I had concrete proof Dza-lu's agents were on site. I parried with how Gunga and I had the situation under control. Neon offered to punch me for that hogwash. I wouldn't have blamed him. Voices were raised, my professional integrity disputed, my future presence in Bloomington, and, indeed, on this earth, repeatedly threatened. I ate several crows. I spilled every bit of evidence I collected from Lady Divine and the courthouse.

What finally mollified him was recounting how I'd spanked Vinnie in his own store. Neon actually chuckled and said he'd wish he'd been there. I left out the juicy details about my tumble with Felicity Goss and gave him the gist of her information on Petey.

"That's everything?" Neon asked after he'd taken a few to let my news sink in.

I raised one hand. "I swear on your father's memory, Neon."

"Don't even go there," he muttered. "Okay, I get why you didn't want to tell me about Angie, but Gunga getting attacked? After you got jumped at the park? Dza-lu is way ahead of us. I need to put people on this."

"Think about that carefully," I said. "How many spare bodies you got with covert surveillance training? How many unmarked cars? Neon, these people are way out of local law enforcement's league. Present company excluded."

He didn't protest. He didn't like it either. "So Dza-lu and Petey Pecorino have eyes all over us, and we're supposed to do what? Twiddle our thumbs?"

The copies of the St. Keyne parchment had ended up on my kitchen table. I returned the set Neon had brought me. "No, we keep following the breadcrumbs," I said. "Even if Nangle was fibbing through his chin pubes."

"About this dragon bullshit?"

I shook my head. "These so-called initials for Walker Chumbley. There's no W in Cyrillic. I don't know what the fuck that says, and I can read Russian."

"Why not come straight out and tell you Kyle was working with the priest?" Neon said. Seeing as I didn't have an answer for that one, he asked, "You want me to go with you to help interview Chumbley?"

I told Neon that the padre would clam up if I brought a cop along. He immediately understood. "Before I head down to Father Chumbley's place, I need to check in to see if there's any word about Angie," I said. "Petey followed Elizabeth Lungs to my office. We can't meet there and I don't want to be seen around the department. What say we rendezvous back here tonight at 8 p.m.?"

Neon hesitated. "You think this place is any safer?" We both looked down at the photocopies.

"For Judge Grange's sake, I hope so," I sighed.

I trudged back across the square to my office. Yesterday's frozen rain had turned to heavy, wet snow, and I hated all forms of precipitation except my shower. An Old-fashioned or five would've smoothed me out along the edges. Maybe tonight, after I met with Neon ...

I almost broke into song when I unlocked my door and saw the answering machine blinking. I skipped through three increasingly annoyed messages from Neon before I heard Gunga's voice. "Howdy, guy," he twanged. "Got me a real nice room out here in the middle of Bumfuck, Nowhere, Hamilton County. Your gal sold you a real bill of goods, Ozzie. Only thing that checks out is Dad having a place in Carmel. I got one more lead to chase down, and it's gotta wait until tomorrow morning. I'll hit up this Lebouche woman soon as I get back to Blooming-gulch, then give you a buzz. You know where to call if you learn anything else."

I waited for another voice. Instead, all I heard was a piercing beep. End of messages. Whoever had Angie wanted to keep me on ice. Frustrated and angry, I went into my own office and sat down at my desk. I jammed my hands in my coat pockets. Along with what remained of my retainer, I fished out the piece of paper with Wanda's handwriting. I dialed the number she'd provided. Lo and behold, some annoyed dude answered on the fifth ring.

"This better be important," he grunted. "I just got to sleep."

Rather than lay some bogus palaver on him, I apologized and identified myself. Told him I was the short, homely guy in a trench coat who checked in the gorgeous Mrs. Smith Tuesday evening.

"How the fuck did you get my number?" he demanded. Hoping I'd never see Wanda again, I said I generously remunerated folks for information, and I'd be happy to come by and drop him a C-note. The motel must've been paying these people jackshit because he instantly got a lot peppier. "What can I do you for?"

"Mrs. Smith may be in a great deal of danger," I explained. "I put her in that room for safekeeping, but I understand she checked out soon after I left. Gave you a story about the room not working out. Did she seem anxious or fearful when she returned the key?"

"No, man, nothing like that," he answered. "Just said she was goin' somewhere nicer. Uppity bitch, y'know?"

I could see Elizabeth Lungs pulling that off. "I know your place charges for all phone calls. Anything outgoing on my tab?"

"Only the room, bud. You were all paid up."

"Did you see how she left? Cab? Anybody waiting for her?"

He had to think about that. "Okay, so's I wanted to watch her shake that hot ass through the door. I turned to hang up her key on the board, and by the time I can take a peek, she's outside. Climbing into this huge pick-up, like one of them monster trucks at a tractor pull." He yawned. "Yeah. Didn't seem like her kind of wheels. Thought it was weird."

I asked if she got in on her own or he saw anyone else in the vehicle, but that was the total sum of his memory. We agreed on a time and date for his pay-off, and I thanked him.

Every so often, when a case completely stymied us, Gunga would announce, "This calls for something unorthodox." Nowadays, the big brains call it "thinking outside the box," but Gunga was way out front of that cliche. He'd introduced me to the I Ching, cowrie shells, automatic writing, and even some proscribed powders we'd fed innocent victims during the MKULTRA days.

I gave it a whirl. I returned to Angie's desk, pulled her discarded blotter pad out of the trash, pressed it flat, and traced the VapoRub smears with a pencil. "This doesn't help," I said. All I'd come up with was a bulbous head with huge almond-shaped eyes. Looked nothing like Dza-lu.

Then my telephone rang.

"Oh, Mr. Yesterday, thank God I've reached you!" Elizabeth Lungs sobbed. "There's been a horrible misunderstanding!"

"You bet your royal blue undies! You've been jerking me around, sister, and there's already one corpse cooling off in the county morgue because of your shenanigans! What the hell is going on here?"

"Please, Mr. Yesterday, you've got to listen to me and believe me!" she pleaded. "Daddy finally came back and he met with Mr. Pecorino. He had the real egg all along! The one I had was a fake!"

"It was, was it?" I said, playing along. "So why was Kyle Fiffie delivering the counterfeit egg to the Pecker?"

"I don't know, I swear, but you must drop the case! I'll pay you whatever you want, but you need to forget everything! Daddy says he can work things out with Pecorino!"

"Yeah, right," I said. "Just like Petey worked things out with Fiffie. The Pecker's got my secretary as well, and I want her back unharmed!"

"Pecorino still has her. She's safe and Daddy's negotiating her release," She hesitated, and I heard another voice in the background. Unquestionably male, but not Dza-lu or the Pecker. A brand new player? "Mr. Yesterday, Daddy and I may still need your help! Can you meet me tomorrow night? Can I come to your apartment?"

How did she even know I had an apartment? Followed the oleaginous trail of Vicks and deli treats from my office?

Gunga was due back in Bloomington by then. He could cover me from my bedroom. As long as I remembered to hide my collection of "amateur" videotapes first.

"Sure, toots," I agreed. "We'll do that. But you better come clean with me, Elizabeth. The cops are all over me like a bevy of starving theropods, and I want answers!"

"Thero-whats?" she said.

Curious question for someone helping to revive a dinosaur. Score a touchdown for team Yesterday.

"Just be here tomorrow at 9:30 p.m. and no more monkey business," I said.

She swore she'd reveal everything to me and hung up.

I once more ignored the siren call of both the gin and the coke, even though I was convinced this whole mess would look a lot better if I got hammered. The Ho-hos were the only food-like substance I'd shoved in my face, and I probably should be stopping up the tears in my hemorrhaging brain with some substantial fatty proteins.

Food could wait, damnit. I scribbled a few notes to myself, trying to diagram the real and possible relationships between all the scumballs involved in the case. Had Elizabeth Lungs been a willing participant with Petey the Pecker from the start? Where did her father fit in? Had Neon endangered Nangle and Judge Grange's lives, not to mention Angie's, with this morning's visit?

I ended up with another whanging headache and a legal pad full of crap that looked more like a Jackson Pollack than an investigation brief. I told myself to look on the bright side of things. After all, this case couldn't possibly get any more twisted.

I was, as usual, dead wrong.

Seven: Hitch Your Dragon To A Star

I hadn't felt so impotent since the security system at I.U.'s Main Library temporarily converted my implant's servomotor into a short-wave radio. For the next week I was broadcasting weather conditions in the Yukon whenever I admired a nice set of parabolas. Under normal circumstances, the smart move would've been to visit Professor Conradt and get the lowdown on the cloning crusaders. Even a hump like Petey the Pecker could deduce that was my logical next step in running his sorry ass to earth. Pecorino and Dza-lu would be packing Angie's giblets in Federal Express envelopes as soon as I set foot near Conradt's lab in Jordan Hall.

I was in a tighter bind than Spiro Agnew in a junior petite leather nun suit. Oh, yeah—that happened, and I got the photos to prove it. Until Gunga and Lady Divine came through with their intel, I needed an angle on this egg scam that Dza-lu might've overlooked. My only option was to play along with Ethan Nangle's silly charade and call on Walker Chumbley, the defrocked priest. Although I couldn't tell at this stage which side of the fence Kyle Fiffie had been riding before he bought a well-aimed hunk of hot lead, I did know that Chumbley would burn his entire collection of Russian operas before he'd willingly align himself with the satanic intrigues of a certain necromancing drug lord.

I took an extended scenic route to Walker's residence to throw off any followers. A generous belt of liquid spine would've been sweet right about now. There was little love lost between me and Chumbley, and I hardly expected a cordial welcome. Some two years prior, my digging into allegations of various unsavory moral indiscretions [KB: see Case No. 99– A Question of Simony or Sodomy?] had led to Father Chumbley's abrupt departure from the priesthood at Our Lady of the Prolapsed Uterus in Gosport. He'd dropped out of sight, with an unlisted phone number and no forwarding address. Didn't mean I had any trouble keeping tabs on the guy.

When I pulled into the driveway of Walker's condo off Sayre Road, I saw that I'd finally gotten a break. The vintage forest green MG convertible in the carport meant Chumbley was home. I observed that the ex-priest had abandoned neither his Catholic nor his Hoosier roots: a Madonna in florid sapphire robes stood blessing a gaggle of plastic geese and pink flamingos gathered around her shelter, an upended rose-hued porcelain bathtub. I was about to yank on the metal bell-pull hanging beside Walker's front door when I registered that the brass handle was a highly stylized male organ. Where in God's gray earth do people find this kind of shit, I wondered as I rapped my knuckles on the heavy oak door.

A solidly built cherub of a man, ten years older than me and six inches taller, opened the door. I have to admit I got a helluva kick watching Chumbley's jovial smile disintegrate into that irritated grimace people put on when they've discovered either a new yellow discharge or an unwanted gumshoe on their front steps. "Hey, you don't look too happy to see me, padre," I grinned, doffing my black etouffee-spattered Borsalino.

Chumbley suspiciously peered up and down his street, then sighed, "On the contrary." He motioned for me to follow him into the condo. "Your arrival was as predictable as death and taxes, Yesterday. I've been waiting for you to besmirch my humble abode." He led me through a narrow marble hallway to a spacious living room with exposed beams and decorated with large tapestries portraying some of the grislier bits of the Fall of Rome. The furniture was spare and Scandinavian. A Steinway baby grand and a pair of speakers as big as capybaras dominated one side of the room. Second baby grand in less than a day. Was I baby grand material?

Walker directed me to a teak Mission-style armchair. He settled into a low beige sofa across from me and sneered, "Normally, I'd worry that you were investigating some addled altar boy's complaints of fissures, dick ... less!"

"There's no need to get nasty, your Eminence," I retorted. "I busted my balls keeping that case hushed up. I'm a lapsed bead mumbler myself, and I told you witch-hunts turn my stomach. Plus I saved you from the Goat-girl of Guadalupe."

"And took a slug with my name on it, to boot," he mused. "Oh, I suppose I do owe you some sort of debt, Osborne. But I'm aware that you may have had a hand in poor Kyle's murder, Yesterday, and I cannot forgive that! Kyle was a very dear family friend, I'll have you know." His voice quavered with anger and grief.

"Let's get a couple of things straight, Father— "

"And will you stop calling me that? Good heavens, quit mocking me!"

"It's only meant out of the deepest respect," I insisted. "First of all, uhh, Walker, I didn't have anything to do with Fiffie getting iced, okay? Secondly, how the hell did you find out I was even on the scene?"

His owlish green eyes darted up to one of the tapestries. "Well, naturally, I called our mutual friend, Ethan Nangle, as soon as I heard about Kyle's death. He'd just been around to your apartment with that nice Lieutenant Knight, who's in charge of the investigation."

"And since Kyle approached you about this valuable missing parchment, I can assume he also discussed his classmate's antique egg," I said. "You put two and two together and guessed that I'd come bugging you about what you told Kyle, right?"

"That's the gist of my reasoning, more or less," Walker replied, giving me a brittle smile.

"Pardon my French, Chums, but that's pure bullshit!" I leaned forward and glared at him. "I'm getting sick and tired of people jerking me around about this rotten egg, Walker, and I'm ready to start crushing some skull! One man's already dead, and someone snatched my secretary to force me to drop this case! I don't like losing secretaries, dig, 'cause Kelly Girls are outta my price range!" I tugged the .38 out of my coat pocket and drew a bead on Chumbley's baby grand. "Either you give me some goddamned answers or else that piano gets it. Have you told anybody else about this freakin' dragon egg?"

Walker leaped up and threw himself in front of the piano. "Good God, man, you wouldn't shoot an innocent Steinway in cold blood, would you?!"

"I'll drill you a new belly-button if you don't spill your guts!" I laughed contemptuously. "Out with it, Chumbley! I don't have all day!"

"All right! All right!" he cried. "Just put away that ghastly weapon! Guns make me dyspeptic, Osborne!" I stashed the pistol back in my pocket but made a big show of keeping my hand on it.

Chumbley began pacing in front of the piano. His Jesuit self-confidence had left him, and his smooth face suddenly looked pinched and haggard. "I've been extraordinarily stupid, I know that, from the beginning. Should've come directly to you the first time I talked to Kyle. Please," he said, holding up his hands to silence me, "don't interrupt, Osborne. I'll tell you everything!

"You called this terrible object a dragon's egg, so you've obviously found out that Elizabeth Lungs obtained the dreaded Egg of St. Keyne. Yes!" he hoarsely exclaimed. "It is a demon's egg, and in coming to me with his copy of the parchment, Kyle unknowingly called upon one of perhaps a dozen people on the entire planet who are aware of the true nature of this dangerous talisman.

"The story of the egg is indeed a bizarre tale, Osborne. Up until 1936, only the keepers of St. Keyne's knew of the egg. The secret of the relic and St. Keyne's deeds were passed down from rector to rector, each man swearing never to reveal the location of St. Keyne's hermitage in the granite outcroppings of Cornwall. Little did they suspect that a Nazi treasure-hunter would be the one to accidentally fall upon that sacred rockery," he murmured in dismay.

"The media and a throng of attention seekers have churned out a million conspiracy theories about Hitler's quest for occult antiquities, but there's more than a kernel of truth buried in all the hysteria. I've seen with my own eyes Vatican documents directing the concealment of various treasures during the Nazis' rise to power. Mother Rome kept quite well informed as to Hitler's diabolical intentions for his ill-gotten hoard. Did you know Hitler seized the so-called Spear of Longinus during the Anschluss? The Heilige Lanze, the bronze weapon which pierced Our Saviour's side?"

"News to me, Chums," I said. "Go on."

"Fortunately for all mankind, the Vienna Spear is a pious fraud. Otherwise?" The ex-priest winced and shuddered. Should I start going back to church and grab a pew? "Himmler was behind much of this occult fascination. He sent an obscure Austrian archaeologist on a mission to scour southern England in search of the Holy Grail. Obsessed by Arthurian lore, Himmler had become convinced that Joseph of Arimathea had brought the Grail with him to Britain. The archaeologist slipped into England and spent a fruitless season combing through the ruins of Glastonbury. He then moved on to

Cornwall, to sniff around Tintagel and Camelford. They've always been more closely associated with King Arthur. How he stumbled upon St. Keyne's hermitage on Bodmin Moor, we are still unsure," Chumbley said, shaking his head.

"'We'?" I asked.

"Oh, believe me, my son," Walker answered, unconsciously dropping back into his clerical mien, "the Church got wind of this filthy Nazi agenda. Learned far too late, thanks to the obstinacy of the Anglicans, but learned nevertheless! What we ascertained was that this brazen thief took the egg from its shrine, along with an equally priceless relic, this parchment you mentioned, which describes St. Keyne's victory over the devil, Kur-ah-desh. The Vatican also determined that the egg never reached Hitler. Its robber fell under the unholy spell the artifact exerts on the undisciplined mind. You see, my son, the egg contains all the wisdom and cunning, every spark of potential vitality of an unborn demon, frozen in stone. Anyone with sufficient knowledge to translate The Song of St. Keyne can tap that power, making it his own!"

"Or hers," I suggested.

"Indeed, Osborne. Hers." He collapsed onto the sofa, his brows twitching with excitement. "After reviewing everything Kyle told me about this Elizabeth Lungs and the evidence I gathered during my studies at the Vatican, I pieced together the egg's bizarre journey to Bloomington. Undeterred by the thief's apparent failure in England, Himmler recruited him for the SS-Ahnenerbe-backed Schäfer expedition to Tibet in the spring of 1938. Dr. Ernst Schäfer and his team were on a mission to uncover the Aryan race's origins in the Himalayas. Himmler's special charge for the thief was to bring back any so-called unearthly weapons and to seek out their "mystical masters." While the thief was willing to bid farewell to his wife and young son, he had no intention of leaving the egg behind."

Walker struggled up from the sofa and started pacing again. I was getting a contact high off of his nervous energy, almost rivaling the effects of that piquant flake in my filing cabinet.

"Almost nothing was known about the Tibetan expedition until after the War, when Schäfer was captured and held by the Allied occupation force for over four years. Schäfer eagerly described his anthropological research on behalf of the Nazis—he was facing charges of being a war criminal. Convincing his captors of his purely scientific motives was the only way to evade the noose. During many months of interrogation, Schäfer provided an explicit report of his journey. The only details of interest to us concern the thief and his fate.

"While the team awaited permission to enter the holy city of Lhasa, our thief and the expedition's photographer, Ernst Krause, traveled to the Yarlung Valley. Only Krause and his Tibetan porters returned. Somewhere in the foothills of Mount Gongbori, the thief found one of these magi Himmler was so fascinated by. This particular practitioner belonged to a reviled school of Tantricism whose adherents consort with all manner of malignant spirits to carry out their evil works," Walker said. Then he paused for dramatic effect. "A disgraced monk, expelled from his temple as a heretic, who was known as Tsi-pa."

"A title reserved for lamas of the dead," I added. "Dza-lu's predecessor?"

Chumbley ignored me and plowed ahead. "Krause did not witness how the thief met his end, but one of his porters accompanied the thief to his meeting with Tsi-pa and managed to escape to tell the photographer a fantastic tale. Upon receiving the thief at his small cave temple, Tsi-pa ordered his devotees to bind him and seize the backpack he'd so carefully protected all the way from Germany. The porter said Tsi-pa removed a globe from the backpack that glowed an eerie purple as soon as he grasped it in his hands. Tsi-pa chanted something the porter could not translate, and the thief began screaming. His groin exploded as if a bomb had gone off in his pants. Mercifully, he died seconds later." Walker glanced at me. "Sound familiar, my son?"

I felt as if I were going to vomit all over Chumbley's Persian rug. "I've seen that trick up close and personal, Fath—uh, Walker. He must have taught that one to Dza-lu."

Walker strode across the room and grabbed me by the shoulders as I shrank into the armchair. "Osborne, you don't understand. Tsi-pa is Dza-lu!"

I shook him loose and tried to chuckle. "You had me going there for a moment, Chumbs. That would make the necromancer, what, over eighty years old by now? The Dza-lu who blew up Neon Knight's father and almost killed me would've been no more than an infant when all this Nazi shit went down."

Walker sadly wagged his head. "You are underestimating the power of Das Eierschicksal, what the thief called The Egg of Destiny. Tsi-pa may have been over sixty years old when he encountered the Austrian, but the egg allowed him to tap into a veritable fountain of youth. And rejuvenation was just the beginning, I'm afraid."

"Still doesn't add up," I said, trying not to sound too desperate. "If this egg is so powerful, how the hell did a little twenty-something like Elizabeth Lungs take it away from him? Not that I'm buying a word of this supernatural mumbo-jumbo."

"Now you're thinking like an investigator again. Schäfer told his captors he wrote to the thief's widow, informing her of her husband's death and how he died. He wanted to meet with her in person after returning to Germany, but she'd left the country by the time Schäfer reached Vienna.

"Osborne," Chumbley said after a moment's silence, "the thief who stole the egg from Cornwall was named Ludwig Abelunge. His son's name was Leopold Abelunge, but he shortened it to Leon Lungs when he emigrated to the States in 1971. Elizabeth Lungs is Leon's daughter!"

"Snappy ending, Walker, I'll give you that. Answers a few big questions, although it doesn't explain how she separated Dza-lu and the egg."

"She didn't," Chumbley said wearily as if I should know better.

"So ...?"

"We know that Ludwig Abelunge took only the egg with him to the East. He left the parchment behind with his wife, Greta. Greta Abelunge had been an Italian teacher at a girls' school just outside Vienna, so she knew how to translate some of the words. In 1953 she showed up at St. Boniface's in the diocese of Groningen-Leeuwarden and asked one of the priests for help deciphering a Latin phrase that, how shall I put this? Shocked his conscience. 'Awakening Lucifer's spawn, Kur-al-desh.' This priest happened to be the prelate's nephew and word got passed. By the time the Vatican saw fit to send the bishop to interview Greta, she was dead of cancer. Her teenage son had vanished." Walker raised his hands. "Taking all of her belongings."

"And in the meantime, Dza-lu flees Tibet when the Chinese invade 'cause even a magic egg can't help him against those odds," I speculated. "Dza-lu winds up in exile in northern Burma. I'm gonna assume he uses the egg to build his merry band of brain-dead tools. Things are going great for Dza-lu until we start hounding him all over the Triangle."

"Then you know what comes next, don't you, Osborne?" Walker said. "Leopold Abelunge uses what he has learned from his mother's translation of the parchment and wrests the egg from Dza-lu. He may have tried to revenge his father's death, but you and I both know Dza-lu is still alive. Leopold becomes Leon, lands in America. Why not?" Chumbley shrugged. "It's a big country with conveniently helpful laws about who can and cannot cross its borders. All Leon Lungs has to do is, heh-heh, sit on his egg like a brood hen and never, ever summon the awesome might within its petrous exterior."

"Just hide the egg?" I asked. "Not use it to hunt down Dza-lu and finish the job for dear old dad?"

Walker leaned his head to one side and made a thin smile at me. "Leon was not an intrepid stalwart like you, Osborne." 'Intrepid stalwart'? Who the fuck has talked like that since Shakespeare? "According to Kyle, Leon told his daughter almost nothing about the egg except that it must remain concealed and never be touched by another human hand. He knew that Dza-lu would keep searching for the egg until he died. According to the copy of the parchment Kyle showed me, those who have disturbed Kur-ah-desh's nest are forever bound as if of one mind. Bound until death. But they cannot sense the egg unless someone else is tapping its energy. That's why Dza-lu has taken over twenty years to locate Das Eierschicksal."

I rubbed my eyes and swallowed hard. "Well, we can't let him get any closer, can we? Did Kyle tell you how Elizabeth Lungs got hold of the egg, or what she was trying to do with it?"

He folded his arms around his head, resting his elbows on his knees. "That's the worst part of this ugly business, Osborne. According to Kyle, Ms. Lungs found out her father was hiding both the egg and the parchment at a cottage he owns down at Lake Monroe. She stole them from him late last summer. She took the egg to Janos Conradt for his expert opinion on what it might actually be. She enlisted Kyle's help to translate the parchment because she'd gotten suspicious when Conradt started conditioning her future in his program on giving him the egg. Kyle told her housemate he was afraid that Conradt might get—"

"Her housemate?" I interrupted. "The Lebouche woman is Elizabeth Lung's landlady. How did Fiffie know her?"

Chumbley paused and stared up at a corner of the living room. "I think he said he met her coming down the stairs from her rooms last fall," he said slowly, concentrating. "That's right! Then he started running into her around campus, and she showed up in one of his music theory classes in January. They became quite close."

"Close as in ...?" I said, putting my right index finger through a circle I was making with my left hand.

Walker pursed his lips and shook his head. "There's no need to be vulgar," he reprimanded me.

"Hey, I ain't the dude with a giant cock on my front door. There's no way in hell Luna Lebouche just happened to keep crossing paths with Kyle. She's as deep into this egg game as Elizabeth Lungs."

"That doesn't make sense to me," Chumbley said in disbelief. "When Kyle told her about the egg and that Conradt was making threats against Elizabeth, she wanted him to convince Ms. Lungs to return everything to her father. If Luna is loyal to Dza-lu, she's got an extremely odd way of showing it."

I didn't respond to that last tidbit. When and how did the Pecker enter into the picture? Was Fiffie working for Wardigus or himself? Was Conradt using his gun buddies as extra heat on Elizabeth?

I was cursing myself for not pressing Vinnie about Timmy Bee and Duane Dorff when I realized Walker was still talking.

"— I tried to impress upon Kyle the untold calamity that would befall our world should Elizabeth or anyone else arouse the egg. He promised he would put it somewhere no one would find it. That was the last I heard from him, but I've gathered from Ethan that Kyle made the grave mistake of trying to fool Dza-lu's subordinates with some other kind of fossil." He sat upright. "I don't have to tell you, Osborne, what would happen if Dza-lu once again possessed Das Eierschicksal. You must stop him at any cost!"

I heartily agreed with Walker on that count. A dank, oily sweat had soaked through my coat. I was ready to gulp down a can of paint thinner to flush out my brain.

After I was sure I'd plumbed the depths of Chumbley Walker's knowledge, I told him to lay low and that I'd be in touch. I dragged my trembling corpse out to the car.

As I drove back towards downtown Bloomington, I struggled to escape this horrendous aura of imminent doom engulfing my soul. If I could just give this hairball a few minutes' quiet meditation, I was certain I'd hit upon a way to straighten everything out. For one split second, I thought I'd broken through to the solution. Then I felt the cold, hard muzzle of a Colt Python against the back of my neck. A thin, reedy voice from the backseat said, "Come on, pilgrim. Vamos or jug a poor player."

"What the living fuck?" I asked.

"Secret message to me from Black Francis. Just pull over to the curb, nice and slow."

My years of experience had taught me not to argue with wackos bearing .357s. I followed my instructions while trying to get a look at this fuckwit in my rearview mirror. All I could see was the tip of a camouflage hooded sweatshirt and the pistol's barrel.

As I put the Valiant in park, I heard an ugly noise that sounded like an instant replay from Tuesday night. It was the crunch of an exceptionally resilient object making direct contact with my unhealed occiput.

Jesus, this was getting old!

Eight: Don't Count Your Dragons Before They're Hatched

Getting hit on the back of the head is real easy. I've done it thousands of times, which probably explains the continuous flow of cerebrospinal fluid from my right nostril and my inability to eat seafood served by anybody named Alphonse. It's that nauseating crawl back into consciousness that bites the big one. And, of course, sometimes you get a bonus out of the deal—you reach back to inspect the damage only to find bits of your superior parieto-occipital lobe oozing over your shoulder. Take it from me, that's no picnic, especially if you happen to keel over into a nest of slavering badgers or a pool of raw sewage. Talk about adding insult to injury.

Thankfully that hadn't happened. Yet. In this chapter.

Whoever had beaned me in my car wanted me back in the world of dragon's eggs and frou-frou cocktail douches a lot sooner than I wanted to return. Rather than rouse me with such timeworn methods as a hearty slap to the face, dumping a bucket of ice water over my head, or running a few volts from a hand-crank generator into the zipper of my mail-order Stretch-O-Comfort slacks, my resourceful assailants had stapled a pair of headphones to my ears. My personal definition of agony was instantly revised as a 250 watt Carver amp flooded my entire being with Ratt's full-volume cover of Donnie Osmond's "Puppy Love." Somebody needed to defenestrate their label's entire A&R department.

I screamed so hard I could feel the gristle in my throat ripping apart. My eyes snapped open and a single bare light bulb blazed into my sweating face. The noise instantly stopped. An unseen hand deftly tore away the headphones. A couple of staples remained firmly embedded in my earlobes. I briefly wondered how I'd explain the new jewelry to my doctor and anyone else I knew.

My head lolled backward and I did a passable impression of a lobotomized orangutan overdosing on barbiturates. My drooling, spastic performance earned me an invigorating lightning bolt in the crotch. So I did have a hand-crank generator wired to my zipper! I can't begin to tell you how much I resented being fully awakened to a cloud of acrid smoke billowing from my groin.

Another unseen figure quickly doused my smoldering trousers with a cool shot from a soda siphon. These guys knew how to entertain their guests, I thought, as the world rudely failed to reassemble itself around my pulsating head.

"Let me guess," I grunted. "You're from the Beta house and I've just been initiated. Thank you, sir. Can I have another?" Somebody in the dark started panting hard. Then I heard a buzzing whine and got a second testicle-fusing jolt to my Sperminator, followed by more spritzer.

"Is this a Valentine's Day present?" I gibbered. "I would've preferred a Whitman's Sampler!" That may have been too reckless. If the voltage toasting my zipper arced to the lithium battery epoxied to my pubic symphysis, it would be Ozzie entrails a go-go.

"Hear that, perfessor?" asked the bone-grating voice of the bastard who'd ambushed me in my car. "This ass-wipe thinks he's a comedian!"

"At least a comedian looks his audience straight in the eye," I said. "Not like the little squirrels who can only act tough when they're sticking a rod in someone's back."

"Give me a few minutes alone with this pint-sized shitstain, sir," a new voice requested, this one deep and deadly. Impersonal. A lot more menacing than the first. Could've had a bright future in retail customer service before he chose junior hoodlum at the jobs fair. "He needs a manners lesson in the worst kind of way."

"Not so fast, Duane," someone behind me softly said. I heard a wet gurgle and smacking lips. There was a hint of an accent in the voice. It only took me a moment to figure out who all the players were. "Mr. Yesterday may yet prove himself a reasonable man. With the right encouragement."

I wanted to shrug my shoulders, but my wrists were tightly tied to the back of a solid mahogany chair. Maybe maple. I'd once again lost the ability to make my eyes blink in unison. Or to distinguish hardwoods. "Try me, Doctor Conradt," I said. "I'm sure we can reach some sort of understanding without Dorff and Timmy Bee rearranging what's left of my cerebrum."

If Conradt was surprised by my deductive prowess, his tone didn't betray it. "Pleased to make your acquaintance as well," he trilled.

"Jesus, it smells like you guys have been guzzling NyQuil in here," I said.

"Shut up!" Conradt snapped.

Squinting a lot got my eyes working again. Judging by all the high tech gear strewn about the large windowless room, I also surmised these camo-clad baboons were holding me in Conradt's lab. Didn't seem like the best place for an extended torture session, but then I'd never attended one of Conradt's classes. Should I ask about the bottles of Ranch dressing with straws in them scattered amongst the computers, centrifuges, and microscopes?

Conradt quickly regained his composure. Or maybe that was the NyQuil lighting up his frontal lobes. "Tell me then, Mr. Yesterday, why do you think I've summoned you here?" he giggled in a surreal, high-pitched voice.

"Smashing me in the head was a summons? Damn, professor, all you had to do was send me an informal memo. Better yet, you could've just called me," I added. "I'm in the yellow pages. Under Ginormous Schlongs."

"Got to have a secretary to answer the phone," Dorff grunted without a hint of sarcasm. His boss did a credible job feigning ignorance about the reference to Angie. Maybe multiple kidnappings rendered him ineligible for tenure?

"Trying to get a rise out of me?" I laughed. I wasn't going to give him the satisfaction. "C'mon, Conradt, you'll have to do better than that. These two buckets of used kitty litter don't have the smarts between 'em to pull off Tuesday night's stunt."

Dorff thrust his mammoth ovoid face into the light. I'd seen larger moving objects, but they had their own moons. "One more crack like that, and I fry your dick, dick." He waved the generator at me. How did he wind it fast enough to zap me without dropping dead of a heart attack? Or without choking himself on the sling of the 9 mm Carl Gustaf M/45 strapped across his immense gut?

"Tell your trained monkeys to quit scaring me, doc. I wouldn't wanna piss my pantaloons and make the janitors file a complaint about Jordan 018," I said. Time to separate the pros from the slack-jawed yokels.

Timmy Bee moved into the light and hauled the .357 out from under his bulky grease-stained jacket. "Let's see how tough you are after I put a round through your leg, twerp," he grinned. "Don't worry. I won't touch your head again. I want to peel off that purty tattoo of Nietzsche. He's my hero. 'Sometimes people don't want to hear the truth because they don't want their electricity turned off.'"

This bon mot met with awkward silence. I almost felt sorry for the poor shaggy dolt. "You spent a lot of time in school staring at a thumbtack and eating paste, didn't you, Beezer?" I asked.

Conradt emerged from behind me and stepped in between the Bobbsey Twins, pushing them aside. "That's more than enough, gentlemen. Mr. Yesterday will be of little use to us if you fatally injure him. We can work out some mutually satisfactory arrangement, can't we, Mr. Yesterday?"

Although Conradt looked like your typical effete snob with his sloping shoulders and shock of unkempt hair sticking straight in the air, his wild gray eyes had that erratic inner light of pure lunacy. Whenever I see eyes like that, I get this uncontrollable urge to grab a pair of red-hot kabob skewers and stab myself some retinas. Might be why I got fired from working security for Sinéad O'Connor in 1988 when she played The Wiltern in L.A.. Or why I never get invited to Deppity Bob's for dinner.

I'd run into my fair share of tunnel-visioned academics during my last few years in Bloomington. Experience and tradecraft had taught me how to finesse these weirdo brainiacs. I'd play the professor as if I was reeling in my second wife's mother on two-pound test—very gently. Conradt's type required the delicate hands of a brain surgeon. The patient planning of a diamond cutter. The negotiating skills of a Kissinger.

"Why don't you go fuck yourself, Janos?" I remarked.

Three quick blows across the jaw with a carborundum-filled enema hose informed me that I'd badly misjudged Conradt's character. I immediately told him I'd be more than happy to play ball. "Your student, Elizabeth Lungs, comes to you with this nutty story about a dragon's egg. She gets all coy and keeps straight-arming you whenever you ask to start work on the sordid MacGuffin. Her song and dance gets stale after a semester, and it dawns on you that she's been using you and access to your lab from the get-go."

"I knew you'd come to your senses, Mr. Yesterday," Conradt said in a voice dripping with sarcasm. Or was that NyQuil? "You see, only

I possess the knowledge of how to tease out the few strands of life embedded in the fossilized remains. My colleagues here have agreed to assist me, and in return, I shall allow them to hunt the first dragon I bring back to life!"

"But something went wrong," I said, playing for time. Timmy Bee and Dorff had made the foolish mistake of not removing my Beatle boots before binding my feet to the legs of the chair. I favored the Paul McCartney models because, while they're the perfect tool for cracking the mandibles of careless punks, they also contain a little sound chip in the heels that plays "She's A Woman" when you click them together just right. The butterfly knives stowed in the backstays might come in handy, too. I was hoping to keep everyone distracted until I could slide my feet free.

"Indeed it did," Conradt lamented. "A week ago Monday, I made a slight miscalculation by getting stern with sly little Elizabeth. I demanded that she turn the egg over to me or I would dismiss her from my program and yank her scholarship. I had not foreseen how attached she was to the specimen. Meanwhile, she starts up this pathetic romance with Peter Pecorino! Nothing more than a ruse to discourage me from pursuing the matter any further. Then Elizabeth compounded her mutiny against me by getting you involved!"

Did I detect the hint of a grin warping Dorff's lipless mouth or was that gas from having recently consumed his weight in KFC? Were there even that many chickens in the western hemisphere? The mind goes down the most random rabbit holes when the gonads are being microwaved.

"Yes, Elizabeth was overmatched the minute she walked in the door!" Conradt tittered. "Totally underestimated me, like every other woman all the way back to meine Mutter! But she shall pay! She shall pay dearly!"

"Interesting theory about Elizabeth, the obvious Oedipal castration issues aside," I responded warily. "Leaves a few unexplained gaps though, doncha think?"

"Gaps?" he bleated. "What gaps are these?!"

Conradt had some deep-seated psychological issues that went way beyond the cough medicine monkey on his back. Nothing a barrel of Haloperidol and behavior modification surgery couldn't take care of, but definitely beyond the scope of a relaxing sabbatical tracking dragons through the rural squalor of southern Indiana. "Welll," I drawled, "what about Fiffie? The cops know for a fact that neither Timmy nor Dorff pulled Kyle's plug. How do you explain that?"

Timmy Bee began misquoting a poem by Rimbaud and a disdainful smile spread over Conradt's pale face. "You haven't had time to do all your homework, Mr. Yesterday! My lads kept a very close eye on Kyle. I've always been unsure as to where his loyalties lay. All that useless artsy-fartsy *scheisse*! As it turned out, I had good reason to suspect him!" He crouched down in front of me and pulled a can of Kraft Cheddar 'n Bacon Easy Cheese out from a holster under his plastic yellow pocket poncho. He squirted a shot between his cheek and gum, shaking as if he'd huffed toluene.

"Kyle stole the egg from Elizabeth Lungs!" he exclaimed, carefully watching my face. "You didn't know that?"

Christ, his breath smelled like dirty feet soaked in NyQuil. I might have to break down and confess everything. "Oh, yes! Fiffie was the author of his own sad fate! He took the egg and meant to deliver it to that lunatic music teacher, P.J. Wardigus. Wardigus planned to ransom the egg back to those ignorant religious freaks in England and use the money to stage her very own production of "Company!" But Kyle never got the opportunity to deliver the egg. He stole that dodo's egg I'd been saving for rejuvenation and tried passing the egg off to somebody else! Before I could get hold of his useless bones, he did me the great disservice of getting himself murdered!"

"How inconvenient," I noted agreeably. "So I take it you want me to turn the egg over to you the moment I find it. Then we'll all be hunky-dory?"

"What did I tell you, gentlemen? He is a reasonable man!" he crowed, turning around to jeer at Dorff and Bee.

I was just about to demonstrate my incredible capacity for rationality by using my liberated left foot to propel Conradt's front teeth through his ethmoid sinus when I noticed a peculiar smell wafting from the louvers around the overhead fluorescent ceiling fixtures. Some preternatural impulse told me to hold my breath. Descending in a thick ochre haze, it was Dza-lu's signature blend of patchouli and lotus flower, masking a neural sledgehammer.

Probably aerosolized fentanyl or propofol. I hoped. Anything but sarin. Dying by nerve gas was a thousand times worse than getting involved with a chick who listened to Stevie Nicks. This wasn't how my life was supposed to end. A hang gliding accident over a candiru-infested river, or maybe a peyote-fueled round of Russian roulette with G. Gordon Liddy, but sarin?

Suddenly all I wanted to do was live long enough to see Osborne Jr. achieve his life's ambition of playing center for the Knicks. Sure, I knew it was a longshot since he was only 5'4". And serving a life sentence without the possibility of parole for bludgeoning his French horn teacher to death with a contraceptive foam applicator. I'd warned my ex the kid would never be able to handle the horn's fussy mouthpiece due to the chronic embouchure collapse he'd suffered after mistaking liquid nitrogen for nitrous oxide. Had that baby sitter with the badly fitted prosthetic leg dropped him on his head one too many times?

Watching in rapt delight as my three kidnappers started twitching uncontrollably and soil themselves, I thanked the gods for an empty digestive system. The professor's eyes turned back in their sockets. He mouthed the word "balls" and flopped over on the scuffed terrazzo floor. Dorff and Bee held out a moment longer, their cyanotic lips drenched in a rich, lathering foam. Or expectorated Ranch dressing. I wasn't about to do a taste test.

By the time Conradt's henchmen collapsed on top of their unconscious leader, I had loosened the ropes around my wrists and kicked both feet out of my boots. I was trying to stay cool and calm. I knew from posing as a teenage Japanese pearl diver that I could hold my breath for at least ninety seconds. I freed myself from the chair with just under a minute to spare.

Picking up my boots, I made a mad dash for the door, but Dame Fortune had other plans for me that night. Dorff's palsied hands still clutched the hand generator and I'd forgotten to disconnect the leads. His arm flailed with one final convulsion. He involuntarily spun the crank just enough to give me a parting blast of electricity. I let out a yelp of pain. That was all it took to absorb a full dose of gas into my bloodstream.

Oh well, I thought, as the floor rushed up to meet my face. Beats getting popped in the head.

The endless black cold must be what drifting in outer space was like. Every nerve had been freeze-dried. Blood the consistency of slush moved at a snail's pace through my hardened veins. I wanted to open my eyes, but the lids were frozen shut. The first identifiable waves of sensory information delivered the sour flavors of incense and anesthetic. It tasted like echidna vomit. That was okay. Echidna vomit actually tastes a good deal better than human vomit, believe me.

Whoever had found me was making fervent efforts to bring me back to room temperature. My savior was tenderly massaging my limbs, gradually coaxing paralyzed muscles to life with a gentle and possibly inappropriate kneading motion. I was more than a bit confused by this new form of medical therapy; the fingers of salvation gradually concentrated their attention on my bionic erogenous zones. I figured I was hallucinating and decided to go with the flow. When the flow took on the attributes of a particularly hot and wet pair of lips, I forced my eyelids apart so I didn't miss the ferocious crescendo.

My first thought was that I have died and gone to heaven. That was also my second, third, and fourth thought, because as I looked down at my recumbent form, I discovered a voluptuous brunette giving me the mother of all tongue-baths.

Nine: Egg Roll In The Hay

Now this is more like it, I thought as the silky point of my nubile rescuer's incarnadine tongue delicately traced the cheesy webbing between the toes of my left foot. I don't care what anybody else says—you get a hundred private investigators together, and ninety-two of them'll explain that the real reason they got into the business is because of the incredible oral action for which our profession is so famous. If you get them drunk enough, the remaining eight will eventually concede they became detectives after they found sleuthing pays substantially better than taxidermy. And let me tell you, Buckley, this babe knew her stuff! She was taking me around the world in eighty ways. She was playing my body like a musical instrument, and her specialty was the old skin flute. It was as if someone had printed a master plan of my artificially enhanced neural net on her tonsils! Her sweet, pouting lips had "pleasure" stamped on them in bright red letters, which probably was a real pain when applying for a bank loan or having dinner with her parents. By her seventh pass over my shimmying corpse, I'd completely forgotten about Elizabeth Lungs and the Egg of Destiny.

Which was exactly what she wanted.

She left my toes squirming in a sheen of cinnabar-scented saliva and returned once again for a fond and comprehensive rumination upon on the Kevlar sheath of my fiercely surging implant.

"That's right, sweetheart," I managed to groan, "shake hands with the Eighth Wonder of the World! Be gentle, though—the shaft may be bullet-proof, but the head is all-natural Grade A corn-fed beefcake!"

Her jaws looked like they were going to unhinge as she completely encompassed my wide world of spurts. She hoovered my meat hose like a starving lamprey. I gripped the rungs of her headboard for dear life as she repeatedly brought me to the edge of darkness at least a dozen times only to stop and stare up at me with a full mouth. Avocado oil from the silicone reservoirs that replaced my Cowper's glands gushed from her nostrils. I squealed, "Ten more seconds of that, and I will go total Mount St. Helens!"

My chestnut-tressed succubus resigned her osculatory grip of my turgid accouterments and straddled my torso. She slid her wet and wooly apex down the rococo arabesque of scar tissue crisscrossing my concave chest. "You are like some grotesque jigsaw puzzle," she said, her sharply honed knees pinioning me to sheets of puce damask. "How is it that you have the body of a man and the loins of an automated donkey?"

"Luck of the draw?" I suggested. My uvula tied itself in knots as I attempted to return her favors and coat her magnificent juggernauts with slobber. She writhed into position, saddled up, and bounced on top of my buttering ram until I thought she was going to crack my pelvis. I'd hoped as I loped towards middle age that I had more endurance, but between a half-hour of skilled irrumation and the added sensitivity from getting my unit nuked at Conradt's lab, I erupted into her love canal after an all-too-brief five-minute ride.

We were both soaking with various bodily secretions, some of mine even naturally produced. She arose to retrieve a towel and wiped off the excess fluids, although a squeegee would've worked better. She climbed back on top of my groin. "That was amusing," she said once she'd caught her breath. "A little too conventional, perhaps."

"The unconventional is okay with me," I wheezed, looking around the darkened chamber for a pack of Luckies. Last night with Felicity had pushed my refractory period to the limit, and I was gambling on the Coolidge effect. "You got any battery clamps and WD40?"

"I've got something even better," she cooed, showing me a small jar of opalescent goo she'd palmed when she grabbed the towel. "Fertile mucous harvested from pregnant Sears catalog underwear models fed a diet of habanero-infused mayonnaise."

"Why not?" I said as she slathered the fiery gel on my instantly revived nimrod. My eyes must have widened to the size of softballs when my temptress rose up to apply three fingers of dippity-don't to her stern port.

"I want to experience you in every possible way!" she wailed, but it might have been the fertile mucous talking. Her face was already bright red and once again covered in sweat. Vicks VapoRub would feel as bland as Mazola if I survived this satanic unguent. I was afraid

91

to look down at my own equipment in case the few square centimeters of original issue derma were blistering.

In my thirty plus-year history of carnal misadventures across six continents (that's right—only six, and anything Phemister tells you about an emperor penguin while we were stationed at Cape Colbeck is total bullshit), I've encountered enough sexual acrobats and savants to fill a Ripley's Odditorium, or, at the very least, a new X-rated season of In Search of... . A policewoman in Brisbane who could grip a stack of five traffic cones with her vaginal walls and carry them across a cricket pitch nearly crippled me that sweltering summer night on the beaches of Moreton Bay. Then there was the so-called Cat Lady of Limbourg, who mounted the handle of a paintbrush on a dildo and twisted her perineum to execute watercolors of her Maine Coon, Whispers, while fellating house guests. I've caught dozens of pussy-launched ping-pong balls in the bars of Rangoon and lost a tenpin match at Holler House in Milwaukee to a 74-year-old armless grandmother who bowled with her iron-grip buttocks. I have even facilitated the profoundly shocking congress of identical twin hermaphrodites from Montevideo and headed the armed team that transported their mewling litter of telekinetic chimeras to a maximum security facility on Svalbard Island.

None of these experiences, however, prepared me for the brunette's prehensile anus. I lay back in stunned amazement as her finely developed levator ani, external and internal sphincters flexed with such perfect coordination that she was able to grasp and tug my burning bug-zapper inside of her all the way to its roots. She smacked me across the face when I began thrusting and commanded me not to move, that she'd do the work. Instead of rocking on top of me this time, she continued milking my poor chili-inflamed giblet plumber using only her internal muscles for what seemed like hours.

"Kill me now! I can't take it anymore!" I remember screaming.

She lunged backward, momentarily bending the delicate engineering of my semi-artificial manwich in half. A horrific stabbing pain shot through my groin. Deeply buried in the base of my flesh-colored unit lay two solenoids that were not designed to meet, and when contact occurred, the electrical current burst from my frenulum to her pubococcygeus muscles. Now, I wouldn't recommend trying this at home without properly grounding your goodies first, but let me tell you, kids, it was the most powerful orgasm I've ever experienced.

After the smoke cleared and the last of our mingled juices sizzled away, I had to warn the ecstatic minx that if she repeated that last maneuver, we'd be the first couple to fry together since the Rosenbergs.

She reached for the jar of hell-ointment again when she finally pulled herself upright.

"Oh, dear lord, babe," I exhaled, "you're not gonna apply another coat of that on me, are you?"

"That depends, you bad, bad boy," she murmured, leaning down to offer me her savory breasts. I was more than willing to suckle on her if that was the price of foregoing another round with the pepper sauce. I would have been content to nuzzle us both to sleep, but I'd clumsily lodged her nipple in the gap between my front teeth.

"Don't you have something you'd like to tell me, Mr. Yesterday?" she winced as she disengaged her left breast from my jagged diastema.

Damnit! I wanted to yell. How could two highly trained operatives both fall for the drugged areola stunt? I gagged on the taste of Dza-lu's licorice-flavored truth serum. I detest licorice and never understood why the bastard couldn't use something nice like butterscotch to cut the bitter tang of his vile potions.

Yeah, it's easy for you jerks to sit back and say, "Idiot sex addict! After Gunga's fleshly follies, Osborne should've known better!" You try to remember every single thing that's transpired in the last twenty-four hours after getting your skull massaged with a gun butt a couple of times, your whopper charbroiled, a lungful of gas pumped down your throat, and then being ridden until you make the sign of the hairy-nosed wombat. Without even paying for it.

"Tell you?" I heard myself pant as my brains slithered out through my own quacking starfish.

"Oh, yes! You'll tell me everything my master wants to know!" she bellowed. She scrunched up her forehead and rolled out in a reverse prostration, disengaging my pneumatic johnson with an audible pop. She jiggled into a fuchsia kimono, pausing to make sure I identified the corrugated scar tissue of Dza-lu's brand on her inner thigh— the indestructible vajra, a ribbed ritualistic club. Dza-lu had sent his Number One devotee after me. Dorje Didax, wanted around the globe for multiple contract murders and dispatching at least fifteen victims by means of what the Journal of Forensic Sciences termed "excessive lubricity."

"Gunga said you were a redhead!" I admitted.

"Give us some credit, Mr. Yesterday," she said. "We've been studying you and Major Phemister for years. We know all of your sickening and depraved predilections. He has a weakness for redheads. Yours is … anything that moves."

Dorje slid a mood-shattering Webley Mk VI out of the folds of her robe and placed it against my temple. It would make a hell of a mess of both her cozy lust nest and my nightlife. "But down to business now. My Lord Dza-lu said we could not carve out your heart until after I'd extracted every bit of information about Das Eierschicksal from this hopelessly tiny brain of yours!" She let the pistol ride down my face and neck. The muzzle came to rest over my right wrist. "I simply adore these eight hundred count Egyptian cotton sheets, Mr. Yesterday, but unless you start giving me what I want, I will blow off your hand!"

"Could you make it my left one?" I pleaded without dissembling. "I use the right one to debug my hard drive."

"You've done that for the last time, lug nuts. Start singing like a good little canary."

The entire case spilled from my lips, but I don't think she heard more than a few syllables. A clanging noise echoed through the poorly lit room, and the lovely Dorje dropped to the floor. Standing before me, a pipe wrench resting on his shoulder, was none other than Gunga Jim Phemister.

"Rough day, huh, chief?" Gunga grinned. "Was it good for you?"

"You're incredibly ugly, and your momma dresses you funny," I unwillingly stated.

He cocked his head to one side, then guffawed. "You dumb sonovabitch! So you got a taste of Dorje Didax's tainted tits as well, huh?" he asked as he raised up his right heel to kick me off the mattress. I could barely move after the erotic Olympics I'd endured.

"Your breath smells like bus exhaust," I admitted. "Sorry, Jim—truth serum."

"Yeah, I figured as much," he said. He'd found my clothes at the foot of the bed and flung them at me. "We better leave ol' Dorje here. Dza-lu's probably got a homing device hidden under her scalp. Or someplace we could only reach with a speculum and vice grips." He aimed his Super Blackhawk at her head. "Permanently revoking her license to honey trap will doubtlessly make my day, but this is your show. Your call."

I wanted to agree with him. "Help me take her back to my office, wrap her up in duct tape and then take a walk around the block while I make mad monkey love to her," I whimpered instead.

"Best not. You're in no shape for that kind nonsense, and I ain't the aiding and abetting type."

"Then immobilize her and leave her. I don't want any more cadavers on my conscience." I retrieved Dorje's Webley and stuck it in my pants.

"When did you grow one of those?" Gunga said. He rifled through an armoire by the door and found a pair of fishnet stockings. Was he enjoying himself a little too much as he hog-tied Dorje while I finished dressing? "You got anything else you want to tell me, Ozzie?"

I clapped my hands over my mouth. "I slept with both your sisters the last time I came down to Kentucky to see you!" I jabbered between my fingers.

Gunga dragged me out through an unlit hallway and into the front room of a rundown bungalow. An unconscious bruiser with a bleeding head was sprawled a few feet from the front door. Too big for Petey. I stumbled off the front porch and registered we were at the intersection of Washington and 8th Street. Dorje had been camping not five minutes from my office? What else had I missed?

"They told me that after they got treated for Kevlar burns and some kind of tropical lice. While we're at it, Oz, who put the pickled wallaby fetus in my birthday cake right before that fiasco in Chiang Rai?"

"Me! Me! Me!" I admitted. Gunga threw me into the backseat of the rented Lincoln Town Car. "I had to do it after you stuck those tiger mosquitoes in my shorts!" The temperature had plummeted to way below freezing. I shivered and cinched my trench coat tight around my chest, squinting out the window. Judging by the sun, it was late in the afternoon. "Christ, Gunga, what time is it? How the hell did you find me?"

"Almost five-thirty, Friday, man. You've been missing close to thirty hours. I got back into town this morning. When I checked your office, there were like a dozen messages on your answering machine from Neon Knight. You totally freaked the kid out when you missed your scheduled check-in with him last night. Took a little guesswork to track down Dorje, but like the constipated mathematician, I worked it out with my slide rule," He glanced over his shoulder. "You might at least say thank-you, junior."

"Yeah, thanks," I muttered. "What the fuck kind of 'guesswork?' Wait— have you been doing Dorje all along?!"

"Dang, Ozzie, you really are saying anything that comes into your head, ain't ya? How else can I use this to my advantage?" he snickered. "Your robocock has been jamming every radio station in B-town for the last hour or so, chief. I haven't heard that kind of wicked static since Cape Colbeck."

"She was the most fascinating flightless fowl I've ever met," I began weeping into my fists.

"Bwahahaha!" Gunga chortled. "Well, fortunately for you, I recognized the noise pronto. Then it was just a matter of triangulating your signal to Dorje's hovel. Glad I didn't creep the wrong joint and that she only had the one lummox guarding the house. Dza-lu must be desperate if he can't find better local talent."

"Yeah, yeah, yeah," I said. "I am so fucking happy to see you, amigo. In way over my head this time."

Gunga nodded as he turned south on College Street. "And then some, buddy-boy. You shoulda checked out this Lungs chick's story before you dove into the septic tank, guy. There ain't no colostomy bag factory."

"What?"

"You heard me, Ozzie. No medical supply business, no father Lungs in debt to Petey the Pecker, no leaky rubbers knocking off coke mules. It seems our Mister Lungs is a pretty slippery little fucker, too. Some kind of European high-roller. Little bird, downtown Indy, told me he's been investigated on a possible Ponzi scheme. Does live up in Carmel, but the neighbors don't have a clue as to what he does." Gunga threw back his head and gave a hysterical laugh that always spelled trouble or a sniping assignment from some grassy knoll. Had he been taking his lithium?

"You're gonna love this, Ozzie," he said gleefully as he pulled into a parking space behind my office building. He turned around to face me. "Old man Lungs showed up in this country in 1971 with his daughter, Elizabeth. Hamilton County court records show he's been sued for unpaid maintenance on an illegitimate daughter. That kid's name is Diana Barreau. Trail on her was a dead end. I poked around a little, talked to Leon's neighbors. My favorite schtick—I'm from Publishers Clearinghouse, and I need to find Lungs 'cause he hit the jackpot. They told me that they hadn't seen him for the last six months and that his maid had been cashiered four months ago. The real trip, though, is where he came from!"

I stared blankly into his fiendishly grinning face and told him he had mozzarella cheese in his mustache. "The suspense is going to make me shit myself, Gunga. Where?"

"The Netherlands, guy," he said. He wiped his upper lip on the sleeve of a magenta velour smoking jacket he wore over his fishing vest and Three Stooges t-shirt. "Holland! The stupid bastard didn't even bother to come up with a different country! I got real suspicious and called the public library to check a Dutch dictionary. Do you know what "Keel" means in English?"

"I shudder to think."

"'Throat!'" he clucked. "And the throat feeds the lungs, don't it?"

"Holy shit! Are you telling me Leon Lungs is Lodewyck van Keel?"

"You bet your ass I am," he answered as we climbed the stairs to my office. "Thing I can't figure out is when van Keel had time to father a second daughter or who she is."

"I haven't come across anyone who looks like another daughter, but he's definitely picked up a new wife," I remembered. "Got an ID on the mother of this other girl?"

"No, name was redacted. I'm betting mom told her attorney van Keel was a scumbag living off dirty money. Attorney did everything to keep his client's location off the record," Gunga said.

"Fuck, she obviously had a smarter divorce lawyer than I ever did."

Gunga made a face at me. "Same here, dipshit."

"Wait a minute! I handled your divorce!"

"I rest my case, your dishonor."

I fished through my trench coat pockets for keys. Gunga handed me the one I'd entrusted to him when I signed the lease. "Anything on Luna Lebouche?"

"Nope, but the stoned goofballs next door to 506 said the house has been quiet for the last week," Gunga said. "There was also a bunch of newspapers lying in the yard. Could've been a week's worth, but I didn't want to call too much attention to myself by getting nosy."

I zeroed in on the answering machine's flashing light as soon as we entered the office. "Maybe this'll be the Lungs bitch, feeding me another cock and bull story," I said and stabbed at the replay button. Skipping over all of Neon's frantic messages, I finally hit a female voice, but it was Lady Divine. She must've tried me while Gunga was breaking into Dorje's crib.

"I've got some juicy scuttlebutt on all three names you gave me," Lady said. "I'm at the club until last call tonight, but you better get here before they lock up because I'm heading to my family's in Cincy tomorrow morning."

"So another late night," I told Gunga. There was one more message left, and this one wasn't from Elizabeth Lungs either. We were greeted instead by the melodious voice of my favorite law enforcement officer, Deppity Bob Slorby.

"Well, you may think you got me handcuffed with your suckin' feds, Yesterday, but this is still my city!" he brayed. "You'd best hightail it down to the hospital, asshole, 'cause your secretary's in the ER. They also got one Peter Pecorino in the morgue. Just in case you give a flying fart about anything besides evading two murder raps, Miss Rodell is just fine. Our friend Petey seems to be minus his forearms. Coroner's prelim says he's been ripening since at least last weekend, so I got a bone to pick with you over how he coulda shot Fiffie! Knight don't want me rousting you before he brings you in for questioning, but then I get my turn. Let's see you wiggle outta this one, motherfucker!"

"You shore got some nice friends up here in Hoosierland," Gunga observed after a moment's silence.

I glared at Phemister. "Have I ever told you that you should change your BVDs more than once a week?" I responded. The truth serum had worn off, but I was in a mean mood.

Ten: Yeggs In A Basket

Dangling from the parachute harness I kept suspended off the balcony of my apartment for those rare third dates, I stared glumly over the top of my frost-dappled coffee. How had I never spotted that pink and chartreuse plaid couch in the apartment across the alley? How was that octogenarian couple limber enough to get in that position? What was it called?

I immediately dismissed Nursing Home Pile Driver. Too generic. Then I realized Maltese Backhoe worked on several levels and poured my coffee on a drunk who'd wandered down the alley from the Bluebird and passed out beneath me. Looked like he needed a bath.

We'd retrieved Angie from the hospital almost three hours ago. My guests had spent much of the intervening time engrossed in the most juvenile forms of horseplay while I tried to establish what our next play should be. When I looked back into my living room, Angie was lying face down on the sofa with her Don Henley t-shirt hiked up around her neck as Gunga Jim applied his so-called stress relief techniques to her squirming form. Much of this therapy involved reaching under Angie's torso and doing something that made her shriek and kick her legs up, catching Jim in the head with resounding thunks. Far from deterring the lecherous Kentuckian, the brutal punishment of Angie's Chuck Taylors only encouraged Gunga to new acts of licentiousness. He stuffed a half-melted Pudding Pop in Angie's greedy mouth every time she belted him.

It was the most revolting routine I'd witnessed since the bachelor party Gunga threw for me the night before my third marriage.

How many years must pass before I could forget the sight of the red panda Gunga had illegally smuggled into the country pleasuring those albino Croatian triplets, the poor, innocent creatures incited to bizarre rituals of lust after having their genitals sprayed with glutaraldehyde? How long would it take before the glutaraldehyde lesions on my coruscated upper palate healed?

Gunga was stuffing the last of my Pudding Pops into Angie's brassiere when I hauled myself up over the balcony railing and said,

"As much as I hate to interrupt Angie's miraculous recovery, I really should ask her a few questions. Neon can only hold Deppity Bob off so long. We need to get our stories straight before I turn myself into police headquarters."

The two flushed faces regarded me with a mixture of contempt and palpable sexual frustration. "Yeah, you're probably right," Gunga grudgingly sighed. He swung off the couch and faltered across my living room in what I can only describe as a pained crouch. He rooted through his duffle bag and whistled at Angie. "I can see that I've almost returned you to perfect health, Miss Rodell. One more treatment, however, is crucial. Have you ever experienced an allergic reaction from having Ben Gay smeared upon your delicate mucous membranes?"

I almost screamed that I never wanted to hear the word mucous again. I had no stomach for where their lechery would lead next. I quietly prayed to the black velvet Elvis painting hanging over a collection of slugs they removed from my body once I'd brought in the Goat-girl of Guadalupe. "Why me, King?" I pleaded.

Angie sat up and adjusted her shirt. Gunga had been belaboring her with a grape-flavored Pudding Pop, and my secretary looked like she'd been using her bounteous chest chattels as a wine-press. "Okay, boss. Fire away. What do you want to know?" She leaned down towards Gunga and murmured sotto voce, "If it's all the same to you, Mr. Phemister, I prefer butter-flavored Crisco."

"Wheee dawgies!" Gunga howled.

I almost said they should compromise and use the leftover Vicks VapoRub in my medicine cabinet, but hewed instead to the straight and narrow. I slouched into my lime green vinyl beanbag chair. "I have a good mind to hang both of you by your ear lobes, but I know Angie would enjoy that way too much."

"That reminds me," Gunga said with a dreamy look in his red-rimmed eyes. "Did I ever tell you about the time I tied a bungee cord around my scro— "

"Later, Gunga!" I thundered. "Angie, could you please tell us what happened after you heard the shot at the park Tuesday night? You got any idea who grabbed you?"

Angie sadly shook her light auburn locks. "Negative, boss. I never saw a face. Somebody shoved an athletic supporter filled with

100

chloroform in my snout. Next thing I knew, I was lying on my side with my hands tied behind my back and my head wedged down between my legs in the trunk of a car."

Gunga, who'd been heading for my kitchen, walked straight into the wall. "Land o' Goshen! We may have to reenact the entire scene!"

"Would you pour some Drano down your pants, Phemister? What about the message you left on the answering machine, Ang?" I asked. "Who told you what to say?"

"Deep male voice," she said. "Cold and blank. Even the guy who prepares my taxes couldn't sound any duller. No accent, either."

"Damn, that eliminates Dza-lu, van Keel and Conradt. Petey as well," I added. "He couldn't do cold and blank if he was drowning in skag."

Gunga came back to the living room with the last of the coffee. "What happened after that?" he inquired.

"I got another faceful of sleepy-sleepy, and then they shoved me back in the trunk. Every couple of hours, someone would pop the trunk to dope me up or pour Mountain Dew down my throat. Put me on a bucket to go to the bathroom, but not often enough. And no TP," she groused. "Next thing I knew, I was crawling around the playground of Grandview Elementary in only my slip. Some degenerate little fourth grader's asking me if I want to play doctor."

"Any idea on the make of the car or where they were keeping it?"

Angie shook her head. "Had me blindfolded the entire time, boss. I can't be certain about this, but I did hear the car doors opening and closing a couple of times. Sounded like Elizabeth's Volvo."

"So persons unknown ace Pecorino and force Elizabeth Lungs to set you up," Gunga concluded. "Someone trying to flush out van Keel by threatening the daughter? Same guy who sent Fiffie to the meet with a fake egg?"

Before I could tell him that I wasn't so sure Lizzy was acting under duress, the telephone by the couch rang. I waved Angie off and picked up the receiver. "Yesterday here," I said.

I barely recognized Slorby's voice. He seemed so calm, so polite, the complete opposite of what I expected after I managed to elude him while we were springing Angie from the hospital. "Oh, Osborne," he said without a trace of malice. "Glad I caught you at home at this hour. I thought you just might like to know I'm here at your office."

"My office?" I exclaimed. "Didn't Knight and Alex Skenitis tell you— "

"Special Agent Skenitis did more than tell me," he continued in that bright, saccharine voice. "Special Agent Skenitis reamed me out a second rectum." No doubt about it— Slorby definitely suffered from a severe anal fixation. Either bad toilet training or an overbearing mother. Probably both. "That doesn't mean I'm required to ignore tips from reliable sources about evidence hidden in a certain scumball's filing cabinet. Before you get all hot under the collar, Osborne, I oughta let you know I obtained a search warrant to ransack your office. Have your ass down here in the next five minutes, and I won't confiscate this book ya got hidden. Some smut entitled *Party Girls From Planet Jizz Meet Rin Tin Wong, the Alsatian Wonder-hound*." He hung up, laughing and pleased with himself.

I tore the cord out of the wall and hurled the phone against the front door. "Something amiss, guy?" Gunga asked.

I made with an evil scowl. "We gotta get over to the office before Deppity Bob befouls $65 worth of spank fodder."

"This your filing cabinet, dickhead?" Slorby sneered at me as Gunga, Angie, and I rushed through the door of my office. He was wearing latex gloves on his hands and beads of sweat on his bloated face. Must've reached page 15 of *Rin Tin Wong*.

"As this poor idiot's attorney, I'll swear that Mr. Yesterday never saw this filing cabinet before in his life," Gunga contended. He peered at the cabinet and said, "Isn't that the one you stole from the Oakland office, schmuck?"

"Oh goody," Slorby grunted. "Now I'll have a matched set of dickheads to hang over my mantle." He gestured at the open top drawer. "Say, Ozzie, you should discuss how you organize your crap with your secretary here. It ain't good practice to keep body parts in with your folders. After a few days, they begin to slime up your papers somethin' awful."

"Yeah, got a whiff of it as soon as I walked in the door. You're gonna tell me that's the Pecker's right hand in there, check?"

Slorby drew out the suppurating severed limb. It looked worse than my head felt. Angie made a low gagging noise and flopped down at my desk.

"I suppose you can explain this one, too?" Slorby demanded, dropping the hand back in the drawer. "Better yet, let me explain it, Yesterday! You and Elizabeth Lungs cook up this big plot to make it look like someone stole the egg so you's can act as her agent and sell the egg on the black market. I know you got the contacts. You make everyone think Pecorino set you up, and they go hunting down Petey. Who you'd already murdered. Only we search Lungs' place and find you've stashed the Pecker's body in the bathtub before you can unload the egg or move the corpus delicti."

Slorby's porcine eyes narrowed and he whistled to himself. It was truly inspirational watching the sorry bastard work so hard to squeeze so many connections out of a thimbleful of gray matter. "Hey, maybe you already sold the egg! It would take a lot of green to swing an operation this big!"

I'd been ruminating on all the missteps, coincidences, and outright lies ever since Gunga had liberated me from Dorje's den of iniquity. Bob's totally erroneous interpretation helped another tumbler drop into place. I replayed my interview with Elizabeth Lungs and threw up my arms in defeat. I collapsed on the BarcaLounger, then noisily proclaimed, "Well, at least you got part of it right, Slorby. Elizabeth isn't involved in my get-rich scheme, but I do have the egg!"

Gunga and Deppity Bob nearly knocked each other over scrambling to throttle me. "What the hell did you say?" Gunga hissed.

"You heard me, Gunga," I declared, pushing him away. "I broke into Conradt's office, found Kyle's locker, and snatched the egg. But I'm the only who knows where the egg is, and I'm not talking until I have it out with my buyer!"

Gunga snorted in disgust, and Slorby smiled so broadly I thought the top of his head was going to fall off.

Before Gunga could start slapping me around, I heard footsteps briskly heading down the hall towards my office. Gunga drew his Ruger and I tugged Dorje's Webley out of my trench coat. We both narrowly avoided capping Neon. He held up his hands and told us, "Easy, fellas. One of the good guys here. Remember?"

"Sorry, Lieutenant," Gunga apologized. "Been a rough few days."

"And then some," Neon agreed. He was holding a piece of onionskin, which he relinquished to Slorby. "You're not gonna like this, Bob," he said.

"I don't think anything short of my mother-in-law's resurrection could bother me tonight," Slorby grinned. His lips moved as he skimmed the report. All of the glee drained from his face. "What the hell is this, Knight? Another fucking shooting?!"

Neon nodded briefly at Angie. "I've been at the hospital, folks. Professor Janos Conradt just got out of the recovery room after emergency surgery," he told us. "He was found shot through the left chest at The Hunt Club."

Slorby slammed his olive drab Stetson campaign hat on the floor. "Goddamnit! Nobody gets shot in my town!"

"Not gonna work as your motto come next election," Gunga said.

"Although The Hunt Club is a mile outside city limits," I happily observed.

"You are dead meat!" Bob blustered.

"Bob, I've already calculated the timing on this. Shooting happened while Osborne was signing Ms. Rodell out of the hospital. He's not your suspect. Again." Neon said firmly. "We found three pieces of brass on The Hunt Club floor. We don't have ballistics yet, but I'm betting they're the same kind of slugs the coroner dug out of Peter Pecorino's corpse. Nine millimeter. From what one of the Club's owners heard when the shooting started, I'm also guessing sub of some kind."

I licked my lips. Things were beginning to dovetail nicely. Now, if only my egg gamble paid off. "Think a Swedish grease gun might fit that description?"

"A Carl Gustaf, you mean?" Neon said. "I don't see why not. Who's carrying that kind of hardware?"

"Bob, I've got bad news for you," I grinned. "One Timmy Bee was holding a Swedish semi on me Wednesday night after he caught me in Conradt's lab. If we can rouse Conradt and make him blab, I'll wager we find out Timmy turned on him. If Timmy's stupid enough to use the same weapon twice—and, trust me, he is—he also told Conradt who he was working for before he plugged him."

Gunga glared fixedly at me. "I hope you know what you're doing, guy," he said. "We're getting into some deep doo-doo here."

That was the most accurate assessment I'd yet heard of this wretched affair. My only hope now was that Elizabeth Lungs left me a special treat in her royal blue hankie.

I put my finger to my lips and jerked my head towards the door. Everyone except Bob followed me out into the hallway. Neon went back in my office, whispered in Slorby's ear, and gripped him by the jacket. I locked the door and managed to lead the crew down the back stairway to the alley without Bob shooting me.

As soon as the frigid air bit into our faces, Slorby exploded like a cheap rubber. "I ain't playin' patsy for you anymore, Yesterday!" He blocked my path to Gunga's rented Lincoln. "I don't care how many FBI flunkies you got in your back pocket! I want some answers and I want them now!"

"Give the man some breathing room," Gunga recommended, trying to step in between us.

Slorby yanked out his night-stick and snarled, "There's one too many assholes in my face, weasel-breath!" Bob tried to say something else, but he couldn't talk too well with the barrel of Gunga's .44 dilating his right nostril.

Phemister held Neon back with his other hand. "Now, I'm real sorry to have to pull a stunt like this, Sheriff. I know it don't feel too nice, 'cause I once stuck a conger eel up my nose on a dare. Got a hell of a sinus infection, but I won back this videotape Ozzie here shot of me and a female manatee at SeaWorld Orlando. I think we all need to approach this deal with clear heads, and I'll be more than happy to clear out your brains real good." Gunga put enough pressure on the Ruger's butt to crease cartilage. "Do we understand one another?"

"Stand down, Gunga," I said. "Bob's right— he deserves some answers." Gunga resentfully popped the pistol out of Slorby's nose. Bob stumbled backward, swabbing his shining schnozz on his sleeve. "Look, we can't waste any more time here, because I gotta talk to Conradt as soon as possible. No matter what Bob's thinking, I don't want to see anybody else killed. The truth is I don't have the egg."

"But you just said— " Angie protested.

"Yeah, Ang, and I'm sorry I had to lie. I put on that little act for the benefit of the duplicitous Miss Lungs and her boss."

"Sense, junior," Gunga said. "Start making some."

"You didn't catch the bug in my office? You're slippin', amigo."

Gunga cocked his head, then flinched in embarrassment. "That blue kleenex between the cushions! Fuck me sideways!"

"I damn near missed it myself until I started thinking about how well-timed Lizzy's phone call was and how Dza-lu's been predicting our moves. I thought it was high time I fed the stinking bastard some old-fashioned disinformation." I turned to my godson. "Dza-lu's been searching for this egg twenty years, Neon. He used it to kill your father back in the Triangle but lost the thing. Gunga and I ran into two of his disciples here in Bloomington earlier this evening. He's going to come after us hard now. We have to prepare for him attacking anyone close to the case."

Before Slorby could interrupt me, I said, "Deppity, I want you and Neon to babysit Angie. I don't know what her captors were thinking when they released her, but Dza-lu will not make the same mistake. We're going to split up at this point, give the bastard multiple targets. The three of you go back to police headquarters. Lock yourselves up in a cell if you have to, but stay somewhere with people you trust. Wait until you hear from me to make a move. Okay?"

Turns out Deppity Bob still had a pretty short fuse on being given orders. He started arguing, but I was fed up with his petty tyrant act. "Were you even listening to me, Slorby? Elizabeth Lungs planted a bug in my office for Dza-lu. He heard me tell you I knew where the egg is. If that monster has his way, your testicles will be packed in dry ice by sun-up and he'll be performing an unanesthetized laparotomy on your wife to make you talk!"

I wiped the sweat off my forehead. Where the fuck had I left my hat? Or the Red Baron, for that matter? "Tell me the best place I can reach you people after Gunga and I finish pumping Conradt."

"We'll hide out in the drunk tank, Oz," Neon answered for Deppity Bob, who was probably still trying to figure out whether or not he'd enjoy watching his wife gutted like a trout. Couldn't blame the man there. Irma Jean Slorby had some major league crazy eyes.

Especially when she implored me to bend her over Bob's easy chair. Made me want to fire up the shish kabob skewers. Hence no dinner invitation.

Slorby agreed with Knight. "We'll be safe enough down there," he said. In a rare show of trust, he gave me his direct phone number. Should I have traded him for the Polaroid of Irma Jean wearing only tasseled pasties and motorcycle chaps? We split up before I could dwell on how that exchange would go down.

After Gunga and I climbed in the Lincoln and headed south on Rogers to the hospital, Jim gave me a disapproving frown. I leaned against the passenger's door in exhaustion, waiting for him to detonate.

"I gotta admit I enjoyed how you managed to piss off both Dza-lu and the local fuzz nuts back there," he said. "You need to remember that kind of cowboying gets innocent civilians killed."

"Keep your eyes on the road, amigo." I looked out the rear window at the mortally wounded opossum barrel-rolling to the curb behind us.

"Oh, damn!" Gunga exclaimed. "We got time to circle back and pick up the little bugger?"

"Since when are you an animal lover, boss?"

"Hey—them's good eatin'!"

"You're worried about Angie and Frank's boy," I said. "Dza-lu's good, but according to Chumbley, he's old and weak. Not to mention out of his element, chief. This ain't the Triangle, 1968. It's only two blocks between my office and the jail, Gunga. Dza-lu won't have time to make a snatch." I smirked at Phemister as he pulled into the hospital's parking garage. "Or are you fretting about your own grizzled hide?"

"Me?" he retorted, locking his door. "You gotta be joking. I'd give your left arm to get a clean shot at Dza-lu, but as far as I'm concerned, this is a private fight between the Devil and us. The Dutchman landing in the crossfire is icing, guy. I just don't want to involve anyone else."

We took an elevator to the walkway from the garage to the hospital. "Don't forget Frank's kid has a stake in this," I reminded Gunga. "I could give a flying fuck what happens to Bob right now."

The elevator doors slid open. Gunga lowered his voice as we walked towards the information desk. "Okay, let's make sure nothing else happens to Angie. She promised to show me how she collects boar semen."

We got directions to Conradt's room and proceeded to the next bank of elevators.

"Listen, Ozzie. What does worry me is that you're doing too much improvising, and you've barely told me ten words about what's going on here. Seems to me you're taking potshots in the dark."

"Amigo, I do believe I've hit the bullseye, even though here's a whole lot of dark out there right now." Before he could backhand me, I said, "Maybe you can help me with a problem I've been having. When you were digging around, did you come up with anything dirtier than usual on the late Petey the Pecker?"

Gunga scratched the back of his head. "Word is he's racked up an unhealthy number of enemies, but I couldn't find any reason for Dza-lu to distrust Pecorino. Much less waste him. A DEA snitch claimed the Pecker took delivery of a big shipment of Triangle horse just after the beginning of the month. Business as usual, far as anyone could tell."

We'd reached the third floor of the hospital and turned right from the elevator. "Elizabeth and her father are playing for different teams, Jim. I'm betting Dza-lu thinks we've been in bed with the Dutchman ever since that fucking disaster in Thailand."

Before I could tell him my entire hypothesis, I caught sight of a white coat heading into Conradt's room at the other end of the hall. We raced down the corridor, huffing and puffing. Nothing to see here, folks. Only a couple of ex-spooks, nearing their expiration date. Gunga badged his way past the police detail Neon had stuck on the professor.

Conradt looked shrunken and frail in the hospital bed, about what you'd expect from someone who'd taken a round to center mass torso. On closer examination, I saw that the thick wad of dressing was up high, just beneath his right collar bone. I didn't notice any chest tubes dangling off his Stryker cart, just a catheter and drainage bag.

The sawbones checking him over was Emily Brindwaker, a thoracic surgeon who'd helped Fesance extract all the lead I'd eaten when the Goat-girl of Guadalupe played riddle-me-this up one side and down the other. "Can he talk, Doc?" I asked her. "Kind of a matter of life and death here. Won't take more than a few minutes."

"Federal investigation, ma'am." Gunga flashed some bogus CIA credentials at her. Maybe once we busted Dza-lu, I'd snag some of Dorje's nipple nectar and finally force Phemister to reveal who he worked for.

"I don't know if you'll get anything coherent from him," Brindwaker said. "It was a through-and-through, so I didn't have him out too long. He's pretty doped up for pain."

"I hate to sound corny, Emily. There are elements to Agent Phemister's investigation which involve a matter of utmost national security," I told her. Not entirely untrue. She put her hands on her hips as if we'd triggered her bullshit meter. "Let me put this another way, doc. I don't want you hearing anything that might require you to interrupt your busy schedule for multiple court appearances."

Brindwaker immediately demurred. "Say no more, Yesterday. Just take what he says with a grain of morphine. He's flying sky-high." Maybe Emily bought our malarkey after all. She closed the door on her way out.

Conradt was barely conscious, and he shuddered when I stuck my nose in his pale face. Maybe it was my aftershave. Maybe it was the memory of how his goons had given me the third degree.

Maybe it was the pressure I was exerting on the free end of his Foley catheter.

"Hep me, *Mutti!*" he moaned.

"I got your full attention, Janos?" I asked. "As you so politely put it, we can work out some mutually satisfactory arrangement, can't we, Professor Conradt? Yes?"

"Yes!" he whimpered. Even with a narcotic drip, the inflated Foley bulb straining against the neck of his bladder must've hurt like hell. So I pulled a little harder. "*Fick mich mit einem Luffaschwamm!* What do you want?!"

"Listen carefully and I can make the pain go away," I said. "Did Dorff blast Timmy too, or do you think Bee is tailing him now?"

Gunga pinched my shoulder. "Get your stories straight! You said that Timmy—"

"Shut up, Jim!" I yelled, shaking him loose. "I remember exactly what I said!" I gave the catheter another tug.

"Aiiiyyyeeee!" Conradt whinnied. His mouth dripped froth and his eyes bulged from his head. Was I enjoying this a little too much? Who knows? Who cares? "Yes! Yes! Dorff shot me, but Timmy wasn't there! I don't know where he is, but he'll hunt that traitor down for shooting me!"

I released the catheter and wheeled on the gaping nurse who'd rushed in when she heard Conradt screaming. "Jesus Christ, don't just stand there!" I told her, cackling hysterically, "Do something! This man is in incredible pain!" Gunga dragged me away by the collar of my shirt.

"I ought to kick your butt over to X-ray and see if you got anything left in your skull!" he complained, tossing me against the wall outside Conradt's room. "Why the hell did you feed us that line about Timmy zipping Conradt and Pecorino when you knew it was Dorff all this time? This stinks worse than a merino ewe in heat! I'm out of here unless you tell me what the fuck is the truth!"

I had just finished gasping out that the voice Angie described matched Dorff's when someone down at the nurses' station called out, "Is there an Osborne Yesterday here?"

Gunga reluctantly released me, and I told the charge-nurse the call was for me.

As soon as I put the receiver to my head, I knew I was in trouble. My ear felt as if someone had poured boiling water into it. Pure evil burned across the wires, searing my flesh. Even in the silence and faint static of the hospital's switchboard, I could sense Dza-lu's ghoulish presence.

"No more games, Osborne," he rasped in a low, malignant voice. "You and my former partner have had your fun, but I grow tired of this child's play. You will deliver the egg, Major Phemister, and your miserable self to me in one hour, or I will begin killing your friends. Colonel Knight's son will be the first, and I will take his soul for my own as horribly as I took his father's. You have deluded yourself into imagining I am weak and impotent without the egg, but I feel it close at hand and my power is returning. I am at Miss Didax's house, Osborne. Be there in an hour with the egg. You know how sensitive I am. If I detect any hint of police activity in the vicinity of this house,

I will call down all the spirits of the damned upon this ugly village of yours! You are aware of my capabilities, Osborne, what tools and resources I command. Do it!"

Eleven: Eggs Benedict Arnold

The receiver fell from my hands and I slid to the floor. Gunga wrenched me up by the armpits. Somebody broke an ammonia ampule under my nose. Dr. Brindwaker tried to stuff an oxygen mask over my mug. I twisted away and caromed off the walls on my way to the hospital lobby.

By the time Gunga caught up with me, I was down on my hands and knees in front of a payphone booth, searching for the quarter I'd dropped. The cops outside Conradt's room must've called security; Gunga was keeping a uniformed dork at bay with his Ruger and squatted beside me. "You want to clue me in on the meaning of that bat-shit weirdness you just pulled?" he demanded.

"It was Dza-lu!" I babbled. "In the flesh, Gunga! Right here in our own area code! He thinks he's beat me 'cause he's got Neon, Angie and Bob, but I've got the fucker by the balls now, Gunga! He's told me where and when, and we are going to send his sorry ass to Hell! I am the Eggman!"

"Would you knock off the nonsense?" Gunga said, helping me to my feet. "And what the hell are you looking for?"

"A quarter, amigo, gimme a quarter!" I pleaded. "Gotta make a call! Gotta call the big cheese!"

"You are cracking up," Gunga moaned, but handed me a quarter from his fishing vest.

I shut myself in the phone booth. I checked my watch, then turned away from Gunga and made sure he couldn't see the number I was dialing. It took less than two minutes and a few harsh words on both ends of the line, but when I hung up the phone, I knew I had Dza-lu precisely where I wanted him.

Gunga followed me back across the sky bridge to the parking garage, bawling at me, calling me every name in the book. He stopped to catch his breath and leaned on the hood of the Lincoln. "That's it, Osborne. I ain't budging until you tell me what's going on!"

"Don't have time for that," I said. I threw open my trench to cool off. "We've got under an hour to get to The Hunt Club and back across town to Didax's house before Dza-lu starts lighting up hostages!"

"Then why the fuck do we even bother collecting Lady Divine's intel?" he fumed. "We'll need every spare moment planning a way to tackle that pillbox!"

I tried assuring Gunga I'd already summoned the cavalry, but I finally had to holler at him, "Just give me the damn keys! I know a shortcut! Lady Divine is sitting right under Dorff's nose, and I'll be damned if I'm gonna let that insane fuck snatch any more of my friends! You can bitch me out to your heart's content, but we've got to make sure Lady's safe!"

"You don't look too hot, amigo," I said, glancing at Gunga's bleached face as his fingers sank into the Town Car's dashboard. "Whatsa matter? Can't take my fancy driving?"

"Me?" he replied. "Naw, I was just wondering how I'm gonna explain those loose chunks of flesh on the grille."

"Don't get melodramatic!" I told him. "I barely winged that kid back there on Atwater. Anybody shadowing us?"

Gunga ignored me. "You lied to me, you bastard! This is the only way out to The Hunt Club!" His eyes widened as he scanned the oncoming intersection. "You plan on letting that eighteen-wheeler get across the street?"

"What eighteen-wheeler?" I replied. I blew through a red light at Third and the 46 bypass, yanking hard on the wheel. There was a horrific squeal of shredding metal. A honking Mack truck cab spun us on a whining 360, shattering the rear windshield and shearing off the Lincoln's rear bumper.

"Cute," Gunga said, brushing broken safety glass off the back of his neck. "I hope you're getting expenses on this caper."

"That truck driver's a fucking menace," I growled. "He's supposed to make sure all oncoming traffic has halted before proceeding through a green light!"

Gunga made a crude jest about his foot and my testicles, but I'm pretty sure he was serious when he knelt down to kiss the asphalt of The Hunt Club's empty parking lot.

I began worrying that Lady Divine bailed on us after the shooting. The cops had blocked off The Hunt Club's entryway with yellow caution tape, and there was a hand-lettered sign attached to the front door apologizing for the unscheduled closing. We jogged around the side of the building. I gasped with relief when I saw Lady's dented purple Jetta parked by the dumpster in back. Somebody had conveniently duct-taped the latch open on the delivery door. I led the way as we padded noiselessly through the rear hall to Lady's dressing room.

We leaned into the doorway, watching in silence as Lady Divine stood over a chattering dot-matrix printer. Lady looked up for a moment, spotting our reflections in her illuminated mirror. She gave an involuntary yip of surprise.

"Jesus, Mary, and Joseph! You trying to make me wet my panties?"

"You betcha!" Gunga leered, sweeping her into his arms. "Ah jus' love water sports, babe!" They gave one another what I considered an overly-long and hot kiss.

"You never greet me that way."

Lady pried herself loose from Gunga and wiped the excess saliva off her lips.

"You're not my type," Gunga quipped.

"That's cause he don't smoke them filthy cigars, Ozzie," she giggled. "Damn you, Gunga, why didn't you tell me you were back in town?"

"Been too busy teaching this goober how to find his ass with both hands," Gunga said.

"Well, he needs all the help he can get. You find Angie yet, fellas?"

I shuffled my feet and studied the ceiling. "You could, umm, call it a case of Amazing Grace," Gunga sheepishly admitted.

"What the fuck you talking about?" she asked.

"She once was found, but now she's lost," Gunga explained. "We turned her over to Sheriff Slorby and Detective Knight. Now Dza-lu's got all three of them."

"Dza-lu? Why are you two ninnies monkeying around with that lunatic again?"

"I'd explain, but we got a serious deadline," I said. Poking my thumb back towards the bar, I asked if she'd heard all the excitement.

"Pretty damn hard to miss," she replied, tearing the print-out from the paper tray. "Happened right on the other side of the wall. Total pandemonium. I never dreamed Dorff would turn on Conradt. Timmy Bee came 'round after the cops cleared out, told me Duane and this Lungs broad pulled a double-cross. Said he was going to ice the rat bastards himself."

"Let's hope we get to them first," I said. "Dza-lu will eat the kid for an appetizer."

"You have time to hear the goods I dug up on these clowns?" she snorted, handing me the pile of fan-fold paper as well as a plain white envelope containing several photocopies.

I glanced at my watch again. "Barely. Can you give it to me in a nutshell?"

"This stuff is strictly off the record, Oz. My contact in the recorder's office could lose his job over this," she warned me.

"Mum's the word." I rummaged through the data she'd just finished printing and passed it back to her. "The Reader's Digest Condensed book version. Please, Lady."

"Well, for starters, neither one of these chicks are natural-born Americans. Lungs' bio says she was born in Burma in '66 and got citizenship in '72 along with her daddy, Leon Lungs. Luna Lebouche is four years younger, and I got her down as the daughter of a Swiss national single mother. She came stateside with her mom, no date for when and no record of a father. Two of them residing in Fishers before mom died in '89."

"Fishers is just a few miles up the road from Carmel," I said. "What are the odds?"

"Son of a bitch!" Gunga exclaimed. "What's Lebouche's birthdate?"

Lady Divine read it from her pad. "April 6, 1970."

"That's Diana Barreau's birthdate! The daughter named in the child support suit I found. Elizabeth and Luna are half-sisters!"

A clot of coffee-flavored bile rose up from my stomach. "Oh, shit," I said. "Their relationship is a lot more complicated."

Gunga must've noticed the sick expression on my face. "How could anything get more complicated, Ozzie?"

"A week before they used fake IDs to buy the house Elizabeth was renting, van Keel and Lebouche got married under the same names.

Poul and Celine Monny. Luna, Celine—whoever—got sloppy and used 4-6-70 as her birthdate on the wedding license application."

Lady Divine laughed and slapped her thigh. Gunga hung his head and whistled. "Shee-it, chief. They're not even from down home in Kentucky."

"If I'd had anything to eat since Wednesday, I'd be barfing my guts out," I said.

Lady was still roaring her head off. When I got annoyed that she wouldn't share the joke, she said, "Neither of you bozos can connect the dots!" Gunga and I stared vacantly at one another. "Selene, Diana, and Luna are all moon goddesses!"

"Fuck me," I said.

"Answer is still no," Lady replied. She continued chuckling and grinning from ear to ear. "You know I came to IU years ago to sing opera, right, Ozzie? Italian opera?"

"What's in Italian?" I asked.

"Poul Monny," she said, "Sounds like *polmoni*, yeah? That's Italian for lungs!"

"Poul Monny and the birthdates?" I said in disbelief. "It's as if the sick puppy gave up trying."

Gunga nodded. "Probably one of those arrogant Continental types who think us American bumpkins only speak English."

"Snooty bastards," Lady agreed. "I'm trilingual."

"I'm cunny-lingual," I said, waggling my eyebrows at her.

"Once again, no goddamn way," she said with a flat air of finality.

"You think Elizabeth knew her sister slash landlady was married to her dad?" Gunga ventured. "That Lebouche was there to spy on her? That's what was going on, right?"

"Hell, Gunga, I'm just trying to process this crap. And how do I leverage it when we meet Dza-lu?" I asked no one in particular. "Are we missing anything else?"

"I don't know if this is any help, but the other big connection between the women is the same foreign bank that sprang for Lungs' fall tuition paid for Lebouche's when she enrolled in January," Lady said. "This bank, Hallum Trust, refused to honor the check Lungs wrote for her fees last month, so she had to apply for a student loan."

"Better and better," I said. "Hallum Trust fronted the money for Leon's place down by the lake. Where he was hiding the egg."

"Hallum Trust of the Netherland Antilles," Gunga grimaced. "It's on a watch-list as a possible funding source for terrorist organizations."

I slapped him on the back. "You slimy turd, Phemister! You're NSA! I knew it!"

"Those motherfuckers? Not for all the gold in your molars, Oz. Besides, I'd have to kill you if you were right." He leaned back on the wall and crossed his arms. "I've been watching Hallum ever since some comrades across the pond made it for van Keel's piggy bank."

Phemister may have been my best and only friend, but at that moment, I was ready to peel off his face. "Why is this the first I'm hearing about Hallum, you asshole?"

"Osborne, you stomped off the playground after threatening to burn guys who wouldn't think twice about strangling their grandmothers," he said. "You're more persona non gratis than E. Howard Hunt and Frank Sturgis, for Christ's sake! I gotta justify violating a no-contact sheet on you every time we talk. You start sniffing around Hallum? All of DOJ and then some comes looking for my scalp. What good does that do either one of us?"

He hung his head. "Look, guy, I am sorry about this. I've wanted the Dutchman as bad as you, but I had to follow protocol." He looked me in the eye. "Maybe we've got a shot at him now, with this nasty little soap opera," he said apologetically. "So let's go get him, okay?"

I still wanted to take him outside and tune him up with a garden weasel, but the shot clock was running. I breathed hard and deep, pulling at my stubbled cheeks with both hands. "Try this on for size," I said once I'd calmed down. "Conradt told me Elizabeth's been putting off delivering the egg to him ever since she initially showed it off in October. She already swiped it from her old man right after fall registration. He cuts her off and goes underground himself in case his former partner comes looking for his long-lost energy source."

"Thus Leon Lungs' disappearing act in Carmel," Gunga chimed in. "The chronology works. Daddy suspects daughter number one of ganking the magic bijou, buys her house, and installs daughter-wife number two as a nark."

"As if Daddy isn't buried in dirt up to his ears, the incestuous prick," I said. "And what's 'gank'?"

117

Lady rolled her eyes in dismay. "Steal. Rob. Boost. Jesus, Ozzie, have you listened to anything on the radio since John Lennon died?"

"What would be the point of that?" I asked. I glared at Gunga. "You're right. Whole scenario makes perfect sense. We are going to have one hell of a treat when Dza-lu gets dragon-egg all over his face."

"For a man who's screwing around with that maniac, you seem awful damn confident," Lady said.

"He'd better be sure of himself," Gunga said, the disgruntled edge back in his voice. "The little Kevlar-plated putz plans to walk right into the viper's nest without the egg. Oh, he claims he knows where it is. Dza-lu'll turn us all into lemur chow in a heartbeat if this scam don't come off."

"I don't think anybody's walking anywhere!" blared a loud, tremulous alto. "Hands in the air and stand absolutely still!" commanded the angry stout woman blocking the doorway. "You're going to pay the piper now, Yesterday!"

"Good evening, Professor Wardigus. I was wondering when you'd show up," I told the deranged music scholar. Talk about bad timing. I warily eyed the 7.63 mm Mauser that she was aiming at my corroded liver. Nice rapid-fire little pistol she's picked up, I thought. Could cut all three of us to ribbons, if the mad Sondheim aficionado knew how to use it. "Still imagine you can hawk the egg to finance your own musical theatre troupe?" I sarcastically inquired. "Better think twice, Doc. There's a passel of mad dogs after that damn thing who'd use your sigmoid colon for violin strings before you could whistle "Begin the Beguine!""

Wardigus quivered with rage, and her inch-thick glasses slipped halfway down her nose. "The egg doesn't mean beans to me anymore! This is curtains for you, Yesterday, and there ain't gonna be an encore this time!"

"Let's not do anything hasty," I suggested. "Where would you be now if it wasn't for me? Need I remind you that I kept the cops off your back over that genital jewelry rubbish? Or that I saved you from the Goat-girl of Guadalupe?"

"And took a slug with my name on it to boot!" she retorted. "It was a different world then, Yesterday, a different show! That was then, this is now, and I'm going to punish you! You and your boss-lady, that phony French bitch, Lebouche!"

"Luna?" Lady Divine squeaked. "Oh, honey, you got termites in your temporal lobe. Ozzie here's trying to find Lebouche! She's mixed up with an international drug cartel!"

"Is that so?" Wardigus shouted. "Well, then, why did he pay Lebouche to set up my sweet Kyle? It had to be this murderer, 'cause Kyle had the real egg, and I just heard this other louse-ridden dog say that Yesterday knows where the egg is!"

"Madam, I will not stand here and be slandered like this!" Gunga said indignantly. "I'll have you know my handmaids dip me in Kwell Shampoo once a week to get rid of the little varmints!"

"Hold on just a second here!" I exclaimed. "This is news to me, Wardigus— how do you know Luna set up Fiffie?"

"Because he told me so!" she howled, great tears welling up in her tiny eyes. Her cheeks flushed, and her small round chin was shaking. "You know what my Kylotchka's last words to me were? He said he was supposed to return the egg to Luna so he

could get Elizabeth Lungs and her friend, Pecorino, off his back, but he didn't trust Lebouche anymore. He thought someone had already killed Pecorino. So he took a real fossil egg from Conradt's private collection to fool them! Then he told me he was going to meet you, Yesterday! And you, you bastard!" she wailed, sighting down the pistol at some of my favorite bits of ersatz anatomy. "You killed him because he'd outsmarted you!"

The final piece of the jigsaw puzzle slammed into place. I danced a jig around the cramped dressing room. Wardigus followed me with the Mauser's barrel, probably figuring it wasn't kosher to drill a man suffering a petit mal seizure.

I was about to make a clean breast of things when Wardigus sank to her knees and dropped the Mauser. Thank God she forgot to take the safety off because it fell pointed at my groin. She was batting at a feathered dart stuck in the base of her neck. Her marble-sized eyes rotated back in her skull, and she flopped on her face. I whirled around to see if Gunga had tagged her with the Xingu blowgun he kept in his boxers. He and Lady Divine had apparently agreed to take advantage of Wardigus' sudden collapse and engage in a bit more amorous tomfoolery.

On closer inspection, I discovered Gunga had toppled face down in Lady's lap. They also had darts jutting from their throats.

Silly me, I thought, grabbing at my neck. So did I. You'd think after letting Wardigus sneak up on me I would've been watching the door. Sober Ozzie wasn't worth crap.

The room tipped sideways and I landed on Lady's make-up table. Would she charge me for the brand new Toshiba I knocked on the floor? Everything slowed to a crawl. I craned around to face the doorway. A gloved hand holding a nifty little dart gun gradually grew into a not-so-little Duane Dorff, all dressed to kill in fatigues, paratrooper boots, and his trusty submachine gun.

"Still playing G.I. Joe?" I tried to say. The words came out as a rope of drool.

Dorff kicked the chair out from under Lady and Gunga and jerked me up by the neck with one hand. Big boy was stronger than I smelled. "The grand poo-bah didn't trust you to show up on time, you fuck," he snarled. "So he sent me to make sure you weren't late."

I wanted to tell him I definitely intended keeping our appointment, but things were getting awful vague and dark. The second-to-the-last thing I remember thinking was my plan was going to fail. Spectacularly. The last thing I remember thinking was, Duane, there is no need whatsoever to sap me with the buttstock of your Swedish K. At the rate these idiots were clocking me, I'd never be worried about thinking again.

Twelve: Hard-Boiled Defective Story

Opening my eyes required just a little less effort than making love to a water buffalo who'd chugged too many cheap diet pills, which is actually a good deal less entertaining than it might sound. The glare of blazing torches ripped my head off my shoulders and sent it on a couple of circuits around the glimmering void. My skull finally got tired of spinning across the planet and crashed down on my neck with a nauseating thud. Somewhere on its travels, my head had snorted a lot of rancid incense and taken a big gulp of aardvark puke.

Because aardvarks eat ants. Ants are chock full of formic acid. That was the flavor in my mouth. So it made sense to me at the time, okay?

My tongue felt like a wad of steel wool, and somebody was doing a bang-up job of ripping my shoulders out of joint. When I leaned my aching head back, I realized I was the one inflicting all the damage— my hands were bound together with a familiar-looking pair of fishnet pantyhose.

I was being held in what felt like the basement of an older house, probably Dorje's place. Coarse limestone walls on three sides reeked of mold and damp and had large bolts driven in at head-height from which hung candle-lit lanterns. A fourth wall made of brick with a massive wooden door stood at the other end of the chamber. Someone had left me dangling from a ceiling joist on a length of chain looped through Dorje's stockings. When I stopped floundering around like a beached whale, I found I could just touch the cracked concrete floor with the bottoms of my scuffed Beatle boots.

"Well, well," I croaked, twisting on my tether to get a glimpse behind me. "The gang's all here!" Dza-lu had assembled a fine cast of characters for his grand finale— lined up against the rugged stone wall stood Neon, Angie, Slorby, Wardigus, Lady Divine, and last but certainly least, Gunga Jim. Everybody had their hands tied behind their backs. One of Dza-lu's thugs must've gotten as tired of Bob's lip as I was and gagged him.

A narrow stairwell leading to an outside entrance separated Gunga from some codger and a young woman I assumed were van

Keel and whatever Luna Lebouche was calling herself tonight. The clothes van Keel and his daughter-wife wore were torn, filthy, and blood-stained. Judging from their badly bruised faces, I'd say someone had been working them over for at least a week. My leading suspect was Duane getting his jollies on the second floor of the house at Prow Avenue.

Nobody looked all that happy to be hanging out in Dorje Didax's custom-designed basement cum torture cell, what with Didax, Elizabeth Lungs, Dorff, the thug Gunga had thumped, and three hooded acolytes slouching on the other side of the room, all armed with assorted semiautomatic instruments of mayhem. Dorje had obviously recovered from Gunga's love-tap. She wore asbestos gloves and was standing by a wood stove in the far corner of the basement, tending a pair of red-hot hedge clippers. I was going to ask her if she wanted to lavish me with some more of that fertile mucous gunk when the door at the other end of the basement swung open.

A stooped, wispy figure clad in nothing more than a frayed orange robe limped into the room. The torches' flickering light and the open stove gleamed off his cleanly-shaven scalp and the tiny silver skulls drooping from his grotesquely elongated earlobes. His face reminded me of an old reptile's body, with wrinkled skin and gray scaly patches. Ancient, flaccid flesh hung from his bony arms, and the fingers of his right hand tightly clasping a human femur were knotted with arthritis. While the loss of the egg may have reduced the rest of his body to a doddering wreck, Dza-lu's black eyes, deeply buried in shadowy sallow sockets, flashed brightly with pure hatred as he drew near me. When he at last spoke, his corpse's voice was cold and quiet, with a British accent.

"I am almost going to be sorry to kill you, Captain Yesterday," he sighed, hobbling in a slow circle around me. "My desire to crush you and Major Phemister has been the sole object of my existence these twenty-three long, draining years."

"Don't go all mushy on me, Dza-lu," I chuckled, more than a little surprised I could speak for the sheer dread that was threatening to squeeze the contents of my bowels down the left leg of my trousers. "You came here after the egg, and you know it. Sure, I got a little sloppy when van Keel's daughter conned me into distracting you from the egg, but look at you. You're ready for the nursing home!"

Baiting the bastard wasn't the healthiest way to trigger my end game, but it was my only option. I had to provoke Dza-lu and force him to expend whatever energy he'd absorbed from the egg's proximity without getting anyone else killed. Riskier plays involved testing the pantyhose's tensile strength and praying to imaginary friends that Gunga Jim was sorting out the rope that bound his wrists. With three acorn squash-size lumps pressing against my posterior parietal gyrus, I was in no shape to try anything besides sticking with my original plan.

"C'mon, Dza-lu, I expected to face a raging dragon, and here you're falling apart on me, old man," I taunted him. "Maybe you've spent too much time napping and changing your leaky adult diaper loincloth to sniff out the jackals in your camp! Is that why you still haven't wised up to Lizzie's scam?"

He slammed his fists together, his thumbs meeting in a classic tantric mudra. "I am not going to lose myself to anger, as you would wish me to," he glowered. "Elizabeth! Do you have anything to say to Captain Yesterday?"

My erstwhile client stiffly bowed to Dza-lu. Then she approached my swaying carcass, pulled off my left boot and holey argyle sock, tossing them aside. Smiling at me, she sauntered over to the wood stove. Dorje traded her the pair of asbestos mitts for a vicious little MAC-10 Elizabeth was carrying. Miss Lungs tugged on the gloves then reached for the glowing garden shears. I was almost relieved when she pressed the flat edge of the blade against the sole of my bare foot. Beats losing anything I wouldn't want to live without, I reasoned as I screamed myself senseless. Probably would have hurt a hell of a lot more if I hadn't damaged my tootsies with a case of frostbite while bird watching in the buff in Antarctica.

After Lizzy finished cooking my foot medium rare, she looked up at me and snapped, "That's for killing my mother, you fucker!"

I could've kicked myself if I hadn't been choking on the nauseating stench of my toasted hoof. Of course! Elizabeth had been the toddler van Keel tried to smuggle out of Dza-lu's Thai enclave. The woman the necromancer blamed me for killing was also van Keel's wife. Christ! I'd been duped by Dza-lu's own granddaughter. And she thought she could hoodwink him as well!

Before I had a chance to do anything with this revelation, van Keel called out to her in a weak voice, "Elizabeth, please listen to me! Yesterday and the other Americans were trying to help us escape this madman! Dza-lu cut your mother in half because she stole Das Eierschicksal from him so we could flee! Yesterday and Major Phemister nearly lost their lives trying to save us!"

A bestial yowl welled up from Dza-lu's skeletal chest. He raised his left hand palm up at van Keel, and gouts of bright red blood erupted from the Dutchman's mouth. He staggered and fell into his other daughter, who tried to support him on her right shoulder. "Please, God, please don't kill my husband!" Luna wailed.

Elizabeth dropped the shears and snatched the MAC-10 away from Dorje before I even knew what had happened. Had she learned how to tap into the egg? Hell, was she the one who'd crowned me at the park Tuesday night? Her head swiveled back and forth between her fallen father and grandfather. "Is this true?" she stammered. "How did my mother really die?"

Dza-lu's drones must've had orders not to harm his granddaughter. No one moved a muscle, not even when she recklessly waved the suppressor at the necromancer.

"The Americans and your father were directly responsible for my beautiful Dawa's demise," Dza-lu replied. "They deceived her with false promises and lies about the life awaiting her in the corrupt west. They seduced her and forced her to betray me! These contemptible animals tried to destroy me by coercing her to take the stone! I was only defending myself!"

Elizabeth kept her weapon trained on Dza-lu. How much clan lore had van Keel disclosed at the dinner table?

I could barely hear Gunga telling Angie, "Family. Never stops being an embarrassment. Am I right?"

Granddaughter or not, Elizabeth's disobedience infuriated Dza-lu. "I will not lower myself to reassure you anymore, foolish girl. You will take aim at your father and his concubine, and you will prove your loyalty to me for Captain Yesterday's benefit!"

Things were not building fast enough, so I tried to pick up the pace. "Hey, that ain't such a bad idea," I told Dza-lu. "But doncha think we'd better get everything crystal clear, ladies and gentlemen? For instance, Liz here may be real keen to plug her old man and Luna 'cause they tried to knock her off for stealing the egg. Luna's none too pleased at the prospect of watching her hubby get aced, but I think the tables'll turn when Liz and Luna find out they're sisters!"

"What the hell are you saying?" Elizabeth's beautiful face contorted into a mask of enraged confusion.

"You heard the man," Gunga piped up. "We have ironclad proof Lebouche is your father's illegitimate daughter. He married her right before they bought your house and sent her to get the egg back." Luna didn't say a word, but I could tell from the look of revulsion that we'd struck a nerve. Where's Maurice Chevalier when you need him to sing "Thank Heaven for Little Girls"?

"He's lying to you!" Dza-lu creaked. "You will do as I command!" Fuck. I desperately needed him to let loose with another bit of legerdemain instead of leaving the dirty work to his gun-toting psychos.

"Since when?" I spat contemptuously in his face. "Our girl Lizzy's been looking out for Number One from the get-go, Dza-lu! She wants the egg for herself. That's why she came to Bloomington and enlisted Conradt's help trying to crack the secret beneath the egg's shell. That's why she got ol' Dorff all hot and bothered over her. She convinced him to assassinate your right arm, Petey the Pecker, to confuse and cripple you. I wouldn't push Lizzy too hard if I were you, Dza-lu. You might wake up on the next astral plane minus your fuckin' head!"

I thought for sure I'd precipitate a black sorcery final round of Family Feud, but all my big reveal just threw sand in everyone's gears. Elizabeth and Luna stood motionless, their brains in vapor lock, while van Keel did his best to meld with the stone wall behind him.

Timmy Bee, God bless his misguided soul, picked this moment to exact his revenge on his ex-partner in crime. He blew through the storm cellar door closing off the stairwell with what turned out to be a Mossberg 500. Then he tossed some kind of flash grenade down through the egress he'd created.

Tensions were already running a little high, what with the extreme group encounter session we'd been enjoying, so I probably don't have to tell you all hell broke loose. I was kind of distracted unhooking my wrists while attempting to avoid landing on my left foot, so I still don't know who shot whom. Gunga and Neon tried keeping track, but they were doing their best to eat floor and protect everyone on their side of the basement. I'm told our other peace officer on site later claimed to have been doing something noble. From what I could see, Bob wedged his bulk under Wardigus and filled his pants. There was a boatload of smoke and human offal filling the air, however, so I might have made up that last part.

Neon reported he saw Elizabeth pivot to splatter Dza-lu and his minions with her MAC-10. Big surprise for her was that someone had loaded the magazine with blanks. The old fart was sharper than I credited and had guessed his granddaughter inherited a heaping helping of his own perfidy. Dorje wasn't in on the ruse—she leaped sideways to protect her lord and master, drawing a bead on Liz with yet another Webley. She fired at Liz and hit van Keel, who, out of some atavistic sense of parental affection, lurched up from the wall to shield his eldest daughter. Luna went into full banshee mode when Daddy Incest pitched forward. She flew at Dorje, a pretty short-sighted move since only one of them was armed and the other one still had her hands trussed.

Dza-lu himself appeared completely oblivious to the maelstrom. Rather than take cover and use his cultists as human shields, he pulled his robe up over his head. He screeched a string of incantations loud enough to be heard over the gunfire. His robe began shimmering with an eerie luminescence.

In the meantime, Timmy and Duane were locked into their savage dueling Rambo wet dreams and not achieving much of anything besides lowering the bungalow's resale value. How two firearms fetishists could sling that much ammo without killing anyone other than Elizabeth Lungs and three of the Dza-loonies remains a complete mystery. To this day no one is sure if Dorff or Bee dusted Elizabeth. Bullets were flying all over the place ... she just happened to be there, that's all.

I had finally succeeded in wrenching the pantyhose loose when Duane comprehended his girlfriend was dead. Dorff threw down the grease gun and charged Timmy. Bee screamed, "That which does not kill me," dropping Dorff with a gutshot from his .357. Gunga had finally wrestled out of his bonds, dove for the Mossberg Timmy managed to lose, and deactivated the oaf by blowing off his left forearm. Gunga swung the shotgun up at Dza-lu, but all five shells had been fired. Dorje pointed the Webley at Jim. I got in the way and wound up with a slug passing through my right thigh.

Within a matter of maybe thirty seconds, Elizabeth Lungs, Luna Lebouche, their father, and Dza-lu's three flunkies all got kicked off the planet. Duane and Timmy Bee spasmed and squirted gore all over the floor. I glanced down at Elizabeth's face and couldn't help thinking what a waste. Her eyes, nose, and mouth were punched in like a smashed watermelon. Then I caught sight of Dza-lu. His robe's weird fluorescence was fading, and I saw bullet holes through the gauzy fabric. None of the slugs had touched him.

Gunga dove to the floor to pick up one of the other discarded gats. He shrieked in pain and immediately dropped the glowing pistol. One of Dza-lu's favorite parlor tricks, I remembered from the shoot-out in Thailand so many years ago. Every firearm in the room flared bright red. Even from a distance of several miles, the necromancer had manipulated the egg and focused its power to ensure nobody grabbed a gun.

"This ridiculous sport is finished! You will now tell me where the egg is!" Dza-lu growled at me.

"How are you going to make me do that?" I gasped. "Stuff one of Dorje's infected boobs in my mouth?"

"Oh, I have far cruder methods!" he said. "Once I have squeezed the breath from your body, I shall smash your head open against these walls and consume your brains! Then I will know all you know, Captain Yesterday, including how you turned my daughter against me!" He extended his arms and stretched his gnarled fingers towards me. The roar of one hundred thunderstorms poured from his toothless mouth. A sickening purple glow bathed his hands, melting the ossified knobs and rendering the skin waxy and translucent.

Without even touching the egg, Dza-lu had harnessed Kur-ah-desh's fury to strangle me with invisible limbs.

The blood boomed through my ears. A million tiny motes of crimson and blue light flashed in front of my eyes. The room quickly shrank to black. I felt my bladder throb and release, and then my tongue bulging from my mouth. I thought I heard Angie blubbering somewhere behind me, but that was probably the last bit of wishful thinking.

Then a vast, noiseless explosion hurled me on top of van Keel's lifeless figure. A column of blinding fire crashed down through the basement ceiling and engulfed Dza-lu. He screamed in helpless rage as the terrifying brilliance swept up his body in an impenetrable vortex. The swirling light chewed back up through the ceiling and the crumbling roof of the house. I could barely detect Dza-lu's flailing form as the light bore him into the starless night sky and then vanished.

Gunga didn't waste a second waiting to see how the last of Dza-lu's goons were going to react. He scooped up Dorff's Carl Gustaf, dismantled the head of the remaining hooded disciple, and used his last bullet to kneecap Dorje. Who says chivalry is dead?

"Worst family reunion ever!" he proclaimed.

"Is everyone else okay?" I hoarsely called out. My ears were still ringing from the gunfire. I couldn't do much more than press my right palm against the hole in my leg while Gunga untied everyone else.

Neon leaped over what used to be Elizabeth Lungs and yanked his belt loose from his pants. "What the hell happened to Dza-lu?" he called out as he bent down on one knee to tighten the belt around my bleeding thigh.

"Whatsa matter?" I remember laughing. "Ain't you geeks ever heard of a deus eggs machina?"

Much to absolutely nobody's regret, I wasn't able to reel off any of the other rancid puns I'd been saving for the conclusion of the Orphic Egg Caper. Whatever the cause—shock, blood loss, oxygen deprivation to the brain, starvation, abject booze withdrawal, or a combination of all of the above—I lapsed into blissful unconsciousness. I was more than happy to let someone else clean up the mess.

Epilogue

Ten days later, I'd recovered enough to join a small, private gathering around a conference table in one of the Justice Building's jury rooms. Doc Fesance had instructed me to stay off both my legs for the time being, so Gunga chauffeured me from my office to the meeting. While I'd mellowed out in the hospital to some of my favorite opiates, Jim, Alex, a pack of DEA agents, and the Indianapolis federal district attorney's office had been employing their considerable muscle and jurisdictional wiles to force all concerned local entities to the sideline. Everyone from the mayor to the chief of police to the dogcatcher was raising hell in the media about getting the hook on the biggest bloodbath in Bloomington's history, but Neon told me most of them were secretly relieved not to get involved.

Judge Grange, who'd summoned the four of us to this cozy little powwow, was not one of those happy campers. In the first twenty-four hours after the gun battle at Didax's basement, Bob Slorby managed to bully the most inexperienced deputy prosecutor in the county into filing an arrest warrant on yours truly, charging me with the murders of Fiffie and Petey Pecorino, criminal conspiracy, suppression of evidence and assaulting a police officer. He tacked on that last one because he couldn't remember Gunga's last name and Neon wasn't telling him. The paperwork on the warrant ended up on Judge Grange's desk. Given the magnitude of concomitant events, Kate the Weight, as I like to call her from a great distance behind her back, was only too eager to sign off, despite her husband's protests.

I would have loved to have been a fly on the wall when Kate demanded that Nangle explain why he had any interest in what happened to me. He was sitting at the table, along with her nibs, Walker Chumbley, and Gunga. Ethan looked as uncomfortable as the judge was furious. She had just finished treating me to a verbal flaying because she had to eat a garbage story about insufficient evidence to support my arrest warrant, which could land her in a possible judicial misconduct beef. Since I didn't want to give her any additional reasons to yank my license, I decided not to tell her she should be whaling away on Deppity Bob. The prick.

Once the judge had vented her spleen, Gunga took us through the "official story" the various feds had woven together under his guidance. The whole shit storm was being written off as a turf war between two homicidal drug lords. Van Keel and Petey the Pecker, having gone underground in perpetuity, made the perfect fall guys. Elizabeth Lungs, Luna Lebouche, and Kyle Fiffie were recast as innocent bystanders who got caught in the wrong place at the wrong time. That was a lot closer to the truth for Kyle. In a negotiated bargain not to pursue murder charges, Duane Dorff agreed to keep his maw shut and take the rap for Professor Conradt's accidental shooting during an argument. I had expressed my own displeasure to Gunga about letting Dorff off so easy. Gunga assured me on our drive over that Duane was scheduled to suffer from a fatal cardiac arrest somewhere between jail and the U.S. penitentiary in Terre Haute.

As for Dorje Didax and Timmy Bee? Dorje caused some serious head-scratching. Immigration and Naturalization, along with every other Justice agency, determined she didn't exist. She might have been somebody's daughter or sister, but she was headed to an extremely dark and isolated future beyond anyone's reach. Forever.

Even though the Beezer had left a prominent dent in my skull, I wound up feeling bad for the kid. He'd been babbling such bizarre crap while recuperating from the missing hock that his doctors ordered a psych eval. The shrinks' conclusion was that Timmy suffered from delusions of an unknown origin. There was talk of naming a new syndrome after him. He believed he was the long-lost love child of Charles Bukowski and Janis Joplin, and that he'd been receiving messages from a nameless chthonic entity encoded in rock lyrics. Haven't we all? Timmy's family agreed to institutionalize their son in exchange for a serviceable artificial limb and a lifetime of government-funded therapy.

What Gunga did not divulge were the identities or the fates of the four corpses of the apocalypse formally in the service of Dza-lu. Probably best for all concerned, (especially you, Buckley), not to know who could be implicated or where the results might have been consumed by future unsuspecting purchasers of drive-in Coney dogs.

With the legal unpleasantries out of the way, Judge Kate softened up a bit and thanked Chumbley for rescuing Bloomington from Dzalu. I again kept my mouth shut. She asked Walker if he had anything to report. He confirmed that both the egg and the parchment had been entrusted to federal marshals and transferred to the British consulate in Chicago. From there, the relics would be shipped to a location to be designated by the Archbishop of Canterbury and MI5.

When the judge asked Chumbley if he had anything to add, he glared at me and said, "I still want to know how you deduced I had the egg and possessed the ability to harness its awesome powers. How could you take such an insane risk?"

"And I want to know how you figured out Elizabeth Lungs and Dorff were behind this clusterfuck!" Gunga squawked before I could answer the ex-priest. Phemister was still honked off at me—he'd been forced to take lead chair on the walloping subterfuge, and all this skullduggery had gotten in the way of his plans for a little three-way action with Angie and Lady Divine.

"Clear as day," I happily replied. "While I was getting my meat stick barbecued at Conradt's lab, Dorff made a crack about Angie's abduction. Conradt wasn't in on the joke, and a few minutes later he bitched about Fiffie taking a dirt nap. That eliminated Conradt. Timmy didn't have the equipment for that kind of planning. The Pecker was already dead. I realized Wardigus was totally off-target when she accused Luna because van Keel couldn't risk anything as public as a hit. Process of elimination gave me Elizabeth and a sharpshooter."

"Ergo Dorff," Gunga nodded.

"As for the egg, Walker? After Ethan here told me Kyle took the parchment to you and you gave me the lowdown on the egg, I couldn't see you letting him go without convincing him how important it was to keep the egg out of anyone's hands. Except maybe a disinterested party with temporal power connections? You were the one person Kyle trusted and, heck, he was Catholic, too. He wasn't giving the egg to Wardigus because she dicked him over and made him take the heat for the Prince Albert heist. All that was left for you was to convince Ethan to lead me to you with that feeble trick of the Cyrillic initials. We talked about us both knowing Russian during our previous dealings.

"The hocus-pocus you performed with the egg?" I glibly laughed. "Yeah, that was a gamble, and a fucking big one. Didn't know if you had the stones to risk your soul and all that bullshit by summoning demonic powers. But I knew what a bookworm you are, Chums. When I phoned you from the hospital and begged you to use Das Eierschicksal against Dza-lu, my only hope was that thirteen hundred years ago, good St. Keyne locked a little of her white magic in that chunk of stone along with the unspeakable evil Dza-lu unleashed."

For the first time in our uneasy association, Walker was speechless. He scowled at Ethan, then at Gunga, who was grinning idiotically back at him. See what I have to deal with, I imagined Phemister telling him.

"That is the most mindlessly irresponsible drivel I've ever heard!" Chumbley sputtered.

"Call it a leap of faith, padre," I grinned. "It worked, right?" I reached for the styrofoam cup on the table beside me and waved it at Gunga for more Dom Perignon. I didn't see any purpose to remaining sober a minute longer, and I happened to know the judge appreciated high-quality fizzy water. The way life in Bloomington treated me, I needed the tough old bird on my side.

"By the way, what exactly did you do with Dza-lu?" I said after Chumbley simmered down. "You're among friends here. I think. Did you kill him?"

"Heavens, no!" Walker indignantly replied. "That would be a mortal sin, his Stygian evil aside. I merely sent him on an extended vacation. If I correctly channeled St. Keyne's beneficence, Dza-lu is now languishing on a wretched little piece of turf in the South Atlantic Ocean known as Bouvet Island. Mind you, he'll get damned cold there because it's covered in a glacier. I took the liberty of sending him on his way without any garments. Hope he develops a taste for penguin flesh. Of course, if my understanding of the parchment was off even by a syllable, Dza-lu better know how to swim. In any event, Osborne, he'll bother us no more. On that I will swear."

"Amen and hallelujah!" Gunga declared, raising a toast to Dza-lu's defeat.

I'd like to say I took comfort in Chumbley's oath, but until I saw the necromancer dead and buried, only a case of DeKuyper's Creme de Menthe and the warm ministrations of a certain Counselor Troi wannabe would help me forget that the fiend would not rest until he had me in his grasp once more.

Acknowledgements

While I had been working on the saga of Osborne Yesterday ever since 1970, nothing really came together until late 1990, when I first started throwing stuff into the void on FORUM, Indiana University's VAX electronic bulletin board. I emailed the rudiments of this book to a few brave subscribers, all of whom had become my second family, and served as inspirations for this and related future projects. My thanks, then, to Gunga Jim Sizemore, Nadine Kwok, Angie Dorrel, Darrin Snider, Robert X. Murphy, Erica Seiffert, Jon Konrath, Christopher Walker, Patricia Ward, Trapper Maxwell, Nathan Engle, Cathy Barnes, David Salo, Dorothea Rovner, Inna Efimova, Miranda Rae Savage, Liorah Rapkin, Lisa Williams, Angie Trambaugh, Pat Cash, to name just a few.

After the demise of FORUM, I eventually found a new home on the alt.tasteless newsgroup. My thanks to my third family—Eric Badofsky, Shelby Taylor, Tony Byrer, Ace Lightning, Deborah Segelitz, Gordon Gibson, Sharon Hitchen, Mary Reeve-Prendiville, Lincard, and Bertha.

Thanks to my sisters, Chris Buckley and Maura Buckley, and their spouses, Cindy Norman and Michael Packer, for their encouragement and support.

My sincere thanks to Jon Konrath (again), for all the advice and for giving this beast a home at Paragraph Line, and to John Sheppard, for his assistance and guidance.

And finally, here at Chez Wombat, love and thanks to Stella, Sidney Junior, Ziggy, and George, for your constant companionship and all the distractions, and to my wife, Patty, for putting up with me and keeping me relatively sane. Love you.

About the Author

Keith Buckley is the author of *The Spy's Report*, *Moron This Volumes 1 & 2*, and co-author of *Indiana Stonecarver: The Story Of Thomas R. Reding*, and *Indiana University Maurer School Of Law: The First 175 Years*, as well as several other works on legal research and Indiana University. He has also recorded more unlistenable music than perhaps any other human being. He lives in Bloomington, Indiana, with his wife, Patty, two Golden Retrievers and two cats. He can be contacted at his business email: 21centurywombat@gmail.com or through his Facebook page.

For more releases by Paragraph Line Books, please visit paragraphline.com.

Made in the USA
Coppell, TX
30 October 2020